"I wasn't bold enough to take her to her bed, but then she, who for all her womanly ways was always bolder than me, took me to bed. Into the bedroom and up onto that high white feathery bed. She stretched out and patted beside her to show me my place, and I went into it. I propped myself up on my elbow and looked down at her and words like hallelujah and glory kept coming to me."

This remarkable novel was inspired by the life of Mary Ann Willson, an American primitive painter of the early 1800s, who settled on a farm in Greene County, New York, with a devoted female companion.

PATIENCE AND SARAH

---

by Isabel Miller

FAWCETT CREST • NEW YORK

PATIENCE AND SARAH

THIS BOOK CONTAINS THE COMPLETE TEXT OF
THE ORIGINAL HARDCOVER EDITION.

Published by Fawcett Crest Books, a unit of CBS Publications,
the Consumer Publishing Division of CBS Inc., by arrange-
ment with McGraw-Hill Book Company.

ISBN: 0-449-23850-4

Selection of the Literary Guild, February 1972

Printed in the United States of America
First Fawcett Crest printing: February 1973

14   13   12   11   10   9   8   7   6   5

To
Miss Willson and Miss Brundidge
who, quite a while ago, lived something
like it, this book is lovingly
dedicated

BOOK ONE

Patience

(Connecticut, 1816)

CHAPTER ONE

One way Martha wanted me out of her kitchen, but another way she didn't want me burning wood to keep just myself warm. Best would have been if I'd died, I guess, but there wasn't much chance of that, not right off anyway, since I lived a healthy country life and was fairly young, and unmarried. Next best was to make me want to die, but I had enough spite in me to want to live, usually.

Martha was my brother Edward's wife. Edward, by the terms of my father's will, was my keeper. I had half of the house and the furnishings thereof, and the use of the central hallway to get there, which shows that my father knew how much help brotherly love needs for the long haul. I had food, firewood, carded wool, summer cloth, shoes, and rides to church spelled out for me. I was to have, always, the milk of two good cows so I could make cheese for income. My father wrote careful instructions for me about what legal actions to take if Edward or his heirs should ever refuse me these things. Their inheritance depended on giving me mine.

But there was nothing all my father's care could do to make them love me.

I think Edward did love me, a little, but Martha had to come first. That was just practical. He had his daily peace to hope for, and his children to protect. I didn't expect him to take my side. I wasn't even sure I had a side.

What made me hard to defend was that I couldn't say what I wanted. I could say what I didn't want, and maybe that's a start but no more than a start. For instance, I was still young enough to think of marriage, at least to a widower, but I'd never noticed that marriage made anybody else feel better, and I was modest enough to know that it would be no different for me. And where other young women could be deceived from having just their parents to judge marriage by, I had what could be called special information: I had Edward and Martha, my age (just about), and close up, and daily.

Well, if a woman's not going to want marriage, she'd best get busy and want to be a schoolmarm or hire herself out as an embroiderer. All I wanted to be was a painter, but how are you going to admit a conceited thing like that to people who are forever taunting you about picking up airs at boarding school? I could just barely admit it to myself.

All winter I'd helped with the work, but there's an air you can have even while working that makes people call you lazy anyway. I'd shelled corn, cut and salted meat, strung fruit, boiled soap, made candles. I do want it understood that I really worked. I'm a little touchy on the point. But now it was January and those big tasks were done. Now there were only the endless daily things, like sewing and spinning and cooking and milking, which couldn't in the nature of things get caught up with, and I wanted a day to myself.

That was why Martha wanted me dead. She didn't get a day, or so much as a minute. "Nobody else has time to make pictures," she said.

"Nobody else knows how," I said, kind of quizzing. I wasn't set yet in my mind to do the picture. It wasn't clear yet, and it had to be. You can't risk paper until it's clear. "Lot's Wife Looking Back" was what I had in mind. It would be fun to catch her just turning to salt, half salt, half woman. Bottom half salt, dress and all. Green tears falling in rows out of her indigo eyes. Lot stalking off sternly, not looking. Then off in the background Sodom and Gomorrah, a little clump of houses, going up in one big flame like a torch.

I looked at the kitchen fire to see again how flames went. A very little bit of blue right at the bottom, and then yellow. "Fire's not red," I said. "Why, for goodness sake, fire's not red!"

"Any fool knows fire's red," Martha said, slaving away. She always became a pitiful drudge whenever I thought to make a picture.

The youngsters sided with me, such as could talk. "Look, Mama! Aunt Patience is right! Fire's yellow!" They only jangled Martha more and didn't help me. She wouldn't look at the fire. She swatted them for sassing and then glared at me to make me feel guilty for getting them swatted.

By then I was thinking about whether to put tiny curtains at the windows of Sodom and Gomorrah, and maybe tiny flowerpots. And should I make people running and carrying things? No, God wouldn't let that happen. If You're going to destroy somebody, You don't let him run out whole-skinned and healthy and carrying something. That wouldn't count as destroying. It would hardly hurt at all.

But already I knew I couldn't do the picture, not here anyway. The walking baby, little Betty, hadn't yet been broken of reaching out for things. Well, I know there's nothing to do about a baby that reaches out but whack its hand, but that's a process I don't like to have to be witness to, and most of all I don't like to be the cause of it, which I would be if I set out a row of bottles filled with beautiful colors. Even a fairly big child, fully broken in, might forget himself and reach out for a sight like that.

I was thinking I might go to my own place and never mind about wasting heat, when the dogs barked and we heard the chain of a sled clanking in the yard. "Ho Buck, ho Bright!" someone called. It sounded like a woman, but it could have been a boy whose voice hadn't changed. Pretty soon there came a knock at the door. Martha went. The same voice said, "Where you want this put? It's the firewood Mr. White asked from us."

"Out front."

"Would you look and say it's half a cord?"

"It's half a cord," Martha said, and slammed the door fast. She was just one thoroughly scandalized woman, breathless but excited too, I could tell, and blushing red. "I never," she said.

Then she couldn't understand why the children wanted to rush right out to see. She whacked them and got them bawling and then whacked them for bawling.

"Who's out there? What's the matter?" I asked.

I'd have got a whack too, but I was just about Martha's size and she knew she'd get a good one back.

"Never mind," she snapped.

With my fingertip I melted myself a peephole in the frost on the window quarrel, but the woodpile was too far around and I couldn't see.

"Is it a woman or a boy?" I asked.

"Never you mind," Martha said.

"If it's a woman, I'll get Tobe to unload that wood and ask her to come in," I said. Tobe was Edward's hired man.

"She don't set no foot in this house," Martha said.

"So it's a she! Do you know her?"

"No, and I'm not about to. I heard about her. That's enough. And I'm not about to have my youngsters see her. This is a Christian home."

I'd heard, too, about Sarah Dowling, and I wanted,

after all these years as almost her neighbor, to get a look at her.

"She'll have to come in," I said. "She'll be here at dinnertime."

"Then she can go home and put a dress on first," Martha said. "It's in the Bible. Not that *she'd* know that."

That roused the children again. They were wild to see. Poor lambs.

It breaks my heart to think of childhood, everybody bigger and whacking and shouting and teaching you not to reach for anything or look at anything, and not letting up on you till you get over wanting to.

I think that when Martha was a baby she had a little less natural interest than some. As for me, well, my father never put his whole back behind breaking me. They say he spoiled me, sending me off to school, and before that he'd made my mother give me candles to read by and draw by, even though they were very expensive in those days. If he was late getting in, she'd never give me the candle, but knowing he was on my side made me strong. If one of your folks will back you up, you don't get broken.

So I guess it was my father, even in his grave, who made me able to stand against Martha when I should have been a timid slave thankful to breathe. My mind cleared and I knew just what to do. I took myself a shovelful of coals from the kitchen fire, not looking at Martha, and with my jaw set I marched myself over to my part of the house and I built a fire in my own kitchen.

It wasn't a kitchen to compare with Martha's. You couldn't cook for reapers in it, but I had no ambitions along that line. The fireplace was adequate, with a good draught. There was no oven, but I had a big iron kettle with a good snug lid that baked just fine.

My father had built my kitchen for me late, when he was drawing up his will and admitting to himself that I

would never marry. I think he didn't want me to. He told
me, during that time, that he'd never met the man he'd
be willing to turn me over to, to obey and scurry for.
He said he'd thought for sure I'd be a boy, from the way
I shook my mother, and when I wasn't his heart nearly
broke for me, wondering how someone with all that go
could stand to be a woman. He said he'd half hoped
naming me Patience would help a little. I suppose I
wouldn't have said all that if he hadn't known he was
dying.

When I had my fire going strong, I sat and looked at it.
Yellow and blue, mostly yellow. And I thought what to
feed this wicked Sarah Dowling who'd enlivened a January
morning for dull Martha.

I should say that this was not by any means the first
time I'd flounced out of Martha's kitchen. The issue had
never before been whether to shut out someone with an
errand on the place at mealtime, but every few weeks we'd
reach a breaking point about something. So I was pretty
good at flouncing, and the main thing is, I had some food
on hand at my place. First time, I'd had to go back in a
few hours to get food. That was hard on my stiff neck
and taught me a lesson. So I had flour, meal, salt pork,
lard, dried fruit, sugar, salt, a few things like that on
hand.

I could have stayed in my own place happily forever,
but, admit it or not, Martha needed me. I'd stay away a
few days, making pictures and sewing, singing little songs
to myself, and then one morning Edward would come
by and say, "Martha's ailing. Can you help out?" so I'd
go back. That hurt *her* stiff neck.

But she ailed a lot and had to bend. She longed for a
real servant, an orphan girl maybe, that she could beat
and that had no other place to go. Edward, with so much
land and a flourishing mill, could have afforded to get her
one. But he didn't think of it himself, and when asked

to he got bullheaded and wouldn't. "There are four women in this house already," he liked to say, ignoring that one was me, and two were infants under five, and the fourth was always on one side or the other of childbed.

When my kitchen was warm enough to make asking someone into it a kindness, I put on my cloak and went out. It was a mean day, windy and bitter, with little hard snowflakes—more grains of ice than snow—driving hard along the ground. I clutched my hood around my face, immediately cold, and hurried out front to Edward's huge, show-off woodpile.

There stood the Dowling sled, weathered to silver-gray like an old house without a trace of paint left on it, and two unmatched mongrel oxen breathing out clouds of steam. On top of the load of wood was a person. I took Martha's word that it was a woman, but I think Martha was very clever to know in a flash like that, especially without looking. I had to study to see the femaleness. But it was Sarah Dowling, dressed just as her reputation claimed, in boots, breeches, jerkin, fur mittens, fur hat with a scarf tied over it to cover her ears. She was throwing wood off the load, fast, making a steady thunder of thumps.

I thought she was snooting me, because she didn't miss a thump when I walked up. I was feeling responsible for Martha and expecting to be snooted. But I only hadn't been noticed. When I called up, "You could put your cattle in the barn," the thumps stopped fast enough. Sarah straightened up and looked down at me.

I like to remember that, how she looked down.

She is tall, and standing on the load put her even higher above me.

Her eyes are a clear bright hazel, and she looked down at me.

She has a narrow longish face. Her hair is brown. I could see a little of it along her forehead, under her hat.

I said again, "You could put your cattle in the barn. They shouldn't have to stand in this for nothing."

She smiled a little, just the corner of her mouth up. "You're not the one I talked to before."

"No," I said. "That was my brother's wife." I had my chin tipped up. In a minute I noticed I had my mouth open a little. Gawking, I guess I was. To end that, I said, "I'm the old-maid aunt."

And that amazing girl up there smiled, a real one this time, both corners up, a big smile, a little too big maybe, a little out of proportion for such a narrow face. A smile like that could break a face in such weather.

"The lady of the house didn't worry none about poor old Buck and Bright," she said, without interfering with her smile to speak of.

"This house has two ladies, so hop down. I'll tell the hired man to take your cattle in and finish up this wood. You're coming in with me to warm up."

She said, "He can take them in, but I got a job here."

She was set. "I cut this wood. This part's easy," she said.

I couldn't budge her. Tobe took her cattle to the barn. I told her which door to come to when the dinner horn blew, and went back to my kitchen.

For dinner we had johnnycake and dried-apple applesauce and fried salt pork and tea. It pleased me very much to see her liking it all, eating fast but neatly. I thought of all the other foods I knew how to make, that she might like too. I wished to make them for her. She had so little the air of ever having been indulged. Surely a few small coddlings wouldn't spoil her or undermine her capable ways.

I was still eating when she finished. She put her cheek against her fist and watched me and smiled at me. I saw where any extended amount of that would give me trouble swallowing.

Indoors, she looked womanly. Lots of women are tall.
Her face is fine and sweet, crowned with a coiled braid.
Her breeches didn't hide how soft she is below. Maybe
they even brought it out. She is also soft above.

"I should admit something," she said. My mind leaped
to ideas I won't tell, but all she admitted was that she
could have finished stacking that firewood and been gone
by dinnertime. "I wanted to see your place inside," she
said. "I never been in such a place before."

"Look around," I said, and finished my meal more
easily while she walked around my kitchen. She touched
my pots, hefted my tools, stroked my plastered walls,
sniffed my herbs, gave my spinning wheel a whirl, all with
such darling curiosity.

"This is fine," she said, without any envy, so I showed
her my parlor and bedchamber too, though they were cold
as outdoors.

I think I had more for myself alone than Sarah's whole
family had, but since she wasn't envious I could take
pleasure in showing things to her.

My pictures were in the parlor, some on the wall, some
in a stack. She was delighted with them. Though shivering
almost as hard as I was, she couldn't stop looking at them.
Nobody since my father had been interested in them, and
when Sarah was I found that I'd been lonesome.

"Look at that!" she'd say, and point to some little part
I'd taken pains over. She laughed at all the little jokes
I'd painted in. It was hard to hide how vain that made
me, and then I thought, why should I hide it, from her?
I gathered up all of the pictures and we went back to
the kitchen and sat on the bench together beside the fire.
I watched her eyes moving to every part of a picture,
and when she smiled or changed expression at all I'd say,
"What's that?" and demand that she point to the part
that did it to her. Besides, I liked her hand, liked to make
her point it.

"I haven't had anyone to look at them," I said, to ex-

cuse my vanity, but I didn't need to because she didn't
hold it against me. In fact, she seemed vain in my behalf,
as though anything good I did was to her credit, and I
began to wonder how I'd been keeping on without her
and without even knowing that she would someday come.

Reluctantly she put the pictures aside. "I got to get
along," she said. "I can't gab all afternoon, like women-
folk." She stood up and looked down at me. "I never
wanted to till now," she said.

"Do you always work like this?" I asked, carefully. I
didn't want to say what other people said. I supposed she
was touchy.

She was far from touchy. "Yup. I'm Pa's boy. He
couldn't get a boy the regular way. Kept getting girls. So
he picked me out to be a boy because I was biggest." Her
voice was so cheerful it made me think perhaps she didn't
even know that she was outrageous.

"Oldest?" I asked.

"No. Biggest."

Cautiously I asked, "Do you like it?"

"Being biggest? There's not much I can do about it."

"Being boy."

"Well, all told, it's best, I expect. Anyhow it seems
natural now. I been at it twelve years. I'm twenty-one
now. I like being outside. I couldn't've fetched the wood
today if I wasn't a boy. I wouldn't be here with you."

"You'll have to change when you get married," I said,
thinking how everyone must say that to her and how she
must hate it.

She didn't seem to. She just said, "Don't figure to get
married," which was what I wanted her to say because I
didn't want that long light step made heavy with child
and that strong neck bent.

"But unless your father's well-to-do—" I began, knowing her father wasn't at all, of course.

"I figure to take up land and make me a place," she
said.

"Alone?" I asked.

Her face got a stubborn look. "I'm strong," she said, and pushed up her sleeve and hardened her muscle for me. I reached up and touched, just a touch. A strong arm, but not a man's.

"Very good," I said, but she saw my doubts and they hurt her.

"I think on going, but I never told it before. I was scared people would say I couldn't. Do you think I can't?"

Let somebody else tell her. I wouldn't.

"No, I think you can," I said, working hard to make my face and voice sincere.

Her smile made my lie worthwhile. "I want to live nice, and free, and snug. I think on it."

CHAPTER TWO

I couldn't get Sarah Dowling off my mind, or even try very hard to. Not even a picture partway done had ever held my imagination the way she did.

I kept wishing I had rubbed grease into her chapped hands. I wanted to even up her rough-cut nails with my little bright scissors.

I imagined her starting west alone with her face all stubborn, walking, carrying a little pack and an ax. She'd go and go. I saw her narrow stumpy road wind up and down. She was too friendly and innocent and natural and pure. She didn't even know that she shocked people. Men might touch her. Women might peck at her with their sharp mean noses. Rain might wet her, animals might leap on her. She would have no kettle and no bed. No thread, no needle, no cow, no cart, no ox, no money. Oh, Sarah Dowling! Idiot girl, stay home, stay here! Why didn't I tell you? You would have listened, to me.

After two days of that I dressed myself warm and started for her. There was no wind. The morning was icy-bright. I liked it. My face wanted to freeze, and when I covered it my breath turned to ice on the wool, so there was that as a problem. But all told I liked that day. It was good to be out, walking along at a good strong pace, breathing the cold air, rescuing Sarah Dowling.

In an hour's fast walk I saw the Dowling place, a small plain unpainted house with a curl of smoke rising. It looked peaceful, but then two dogs came rushing out in full cry. Not mean or anything, just taking care of their place, but that was the end of peace. I may have been their first female visitor. The door opened. A tall woman crowded by girls looked out at me. Her arms were folded across her front. She nodded cautiously. The girls just stared. Bright Dowling eyes, hazel, none Sarah's. It seemed dimly presumptuous of those girls to look so much like Sarah.

I managed to outshout the dogs and make Mrs. Dowling understand that I'd come to see Sarah. A lull in the barking let me hear "She's in the clearing."

All five girls wanted to lead me to her. It wasn't easy to convince them that I could see tracks in snow as well as anyone, but at last they pointed me right and left the rest to me.

I found Sarah's trail with no trouble and set my feet in her big tracks. I had to stretch to step from one to the next. Pretty soon I began to hear her ax, but I didn't look up because I was working at my walking, and whispering, "No plow, no scissors, no basket, no rake, you can't, you can't."

The ax stopped and I looked up and there she was, surprised and smiling, leaning on her hand against a tree. The sight of her rocked me some, because nobody really looked like her after all, and I was a little tired anyway, so I leaned back against a different tree, nearby.

"Patience White!" she said, with a face so glad I didn't see how I could say my piece even though it was for her good. How be flat and sensible when someone's so glad to see you?

She left her ax hanging by its blade in the good big beech she was girdling, and went to brush the snow off a log to make me a seat. Hard snow still clung in the ridges of the bark, so she took her mittens off and laid them together there.

"Here," she said, but I didn't like to sit when she didn't, or see her go barehanded for my sake, so I stayed standing.

I picked up her mittens, which were fur on the backs but plain leather on the palms. "Did you wear it off or did they start this way?" I asked. When she didn't answer, I came to notice that I was pressing them to my face. She watched me, and I felt I had to explain. "They feel good," I said. "Like a kitten," which was only partly true—they were bearskin and very coarse, but they did feel good. "Here, put them back on."

"They started this way," she said, slipping them over her red hands. "You can't grip an ax with fur."

That gave me what I chose to consider a natural opportunity to say what I'd come for. "Is that your ax?" I asked. "Your own ax?"

"Why, I don't know. It's one of our axes. I guess it's mine. It's the one I use."

"But could you take it pioneering with you?"

"I should think Pa'd give me that much," she said, uncertain already.

I should have been glad that my task was easy, but I was unexpectedly sad. I would have felt better for both our sakes if I could have hugged her in the commonplace way of women together, but something about her made me unable even to hold her hand to comfort us. She didn't do woman things. I kept my distance.

"Sarah Dowling, dear," I said. "Dear Sarah Dowling. How reasonable are you being? How many details have you thought out?"

"I won't tell you." Her tone reminded me that she was six years younger than I. "You'd just say I couldn't."

"I feel I must say it, dear."

"I thought you was my friend," she said. So young.

"I am your friend. That's why I feel I have to. You might not heed anyone else."

She scowled at me. "I won't heed you, neither." Her uncertainty departed. She strode furiously around her little clearing of trampled snow and chips. "I'm going. I'm going. I'm strong. I can do it."

"I wish you wouldn't."

"You're not my friend when you want me to stay here. Where even my ax ain't mine. Look!" She seized the ax and with two strokes broke a big chip from the beech. "It's mine because I can do that with it. That makes it mine." She was breathing hard. "You want me to get married."

"No, I don't."

As though I hadn't spoken, she said, "Well, I won't. I don't have to. I won't. I'm going."

"Where are you going?"

"I won't tell you."

"Do you have any money?"

"I'll buy my land like Pa's buying his. Land buys itself, with wood and ashes and oats and corn."

"Do you think—dear—that anyone would let a woman alone, with no money, take an indenture on this land?"

"They don't have to know I'm a woman."

I bowed my head to take that in. When I looked again she had her back to me. "Well, what'd you think?" she asked without turning. "That I was going to drag out there in a skirt? What'd you think?"

If only she'd been like other girls so I could have gone up to her and put my arms around her!

I said, "I doubt anyone would let a man alone do it, either. One alone's not enough. You haven't thought."

"I have thought," she said, still not turning, but tipping her head back, looking up into the treetops. "I'll tell you what I've thought. I've thought I'd rather die than not go." She turned around then and let me see her face. "I have to try," she said.

And I knew that Columbus looked like that and said that.

"Then take me with you," I said.

As soon as I said it, I knew it was what I'd intended, unknown to myself all along. My words stayed in the air and I listened to them again. They sounded even more reasonable and natural.

But Sarah said, "You better think it over."

"I've been thinking. I just didn't know it. I've thought of all the things we'll need, that I can bring. I've got two cows. Don't you need my cows?"

"Course I do. But you think some more."

I knew she'd let me go with her, and that she was only trying to play man, all slow and steady, not impulsive, weighing carefully. I was amused but didn't say so. Time enough later to teach her that it's better to be a real woman than an imitation man, and that when someone chooses a woman to go away with it's because a woman is what's preferred.

I said, "I want to make pictures where nobody's angry at me for it." I thought if I put it in terms of my own needs, she'd give in easier.

"I wouldn't be angry," she said. "I'd be proud."

"Yes, I know you would."

There was quiet then. I can't tell what she did or how she looked because I was watching my toe push chips into a pattern.

Then she said, "I'll come by your place Sunday and you tell me then if you haven't changed your mind."

"I won't have."

"I wanted to start at the end of March, but if we're taking cattle we've got to wait for grass. That puts it off a month."

"Sarah Dowling, you act like I've made you a problem. You could act a little glad."

"Well, you might not like it out there. You don't know what it is to live hard."

"If I don't like it, I won't stay."

"That's what I'm scared of."

"If I don't stay, you'll be alone, just as you would have been anyway. Where are we going?"

"York State."

"Yes, but where there?"

"Genesee. The Genesee country."

"So far?"

"There's a good road."

"A toll road. But I'll have money."

"Pa's got brothers out there. They'll help us."

My spirit dropped at the thought of any help except what we would give each other. "Let's go somewhere else then," I said.

"Everybody goes where they've got kin. Who'll shelter us but kin while we build our house? Who'll roll up the logs for our house? Who'll help us raise our roof? Who'll feed us while we wait for our crops?"

"I guess I just don't like kin much," I said, sulking. "I thought we'd do everything for ourselves."

She laughed. "Don't worry, it'll be hard enough. It'll exercise us. If you still say the same thing Sunday."

I was so put-off I came near to telling her that *I* was raised to call that day Sabbath.

Along about Friday, Martha took sick. Edward came by to tell me so and ask me back. I was working on Lot's Wife, enjoying myself, but for the first time I didn't mind going back because I knew it wasn't my fate anymore. Edward was expecting me to mind, though, so he didn't notice that I didn't. He was grumpy, at Martha for being sick (as she was carrying a child), at me for not doing my part, at the general make and trend of the world.

"Pa didn't mean you to do nothing," he said.

"Brother, what would you give to be rid of me?"

"Don't talk looney. Just come on."

"I will sell out reasonable and be on my way to Genesee," I said. I was corking my color bottles carefully, acting mostly interested in them. The main thing was to set him thinking.

"You could get Martha some steady help. A man of your means should anyway. And the whole house would be yours."

"Just come on," he said.

"I'll be there in a minute."

He should have left then, but I had his attention. He didn't want to show that I did, so he didn't ask any questions.

I laughed. "Run along, Brother. I'll be there."

He frowned and stomped off.

Martha was on a pallet in the kitchen where she could keep watch. She looked away when I went in. The children were clustered timidly around her, so quiet and good. Afraid their mother was dying, I think. Afraid of something as big and terrible as that. And of course it was certain that one such time she would be. If not this time, the twelfth or twentieth; Edward would fill her as often as necessary.

I felt the sadness the children always made me feel, but something new too—something for Martha.

I thought what it would be, to live her life.

"Did you eat?" I asked her gently. And being gentle made me remember a dream from the night before. In the dream, Martha's bosom was bare and I went, very afraid but full of longing, and put my mouth against it. I expected her to push me away, but instead I felt her hand on the back of my head, pressing me close, and she murmured, "Of course, of course."

I wonder if that dream would have changed me even if I hadn't remembered it. Remembering it made the end of a time in my heart.

Martha looked so puzzled, and I asked again, "Did you eat?"—ashamed that so simple a human thing from me could puzzle her.

She shook her head. "I couldn't," she whispered, and I saw that her eyes were full. I knelt down on her pallet and held her face against my shoulder, wondering why this had stopped being possible and why it was easy now.

I poached an egg in milk for her and watched her eat it. I remembered something I tended to forget, that Martha had been my friend first. She came to our house because she liked me, to see me, and then she saw Edward and liked him better. I think if I'd found words for how I felt when that happened, they would have been, "You chose him—now choke on him."

Strange not to have the words until they're not true anymore.

I wondered how much sooner there might have been a way to live our days, or if there was a rule that you can't see the way until the end.

Because Martha and I were ended. I was going with Sarah to feed her and hold her head against me when she was sad and knead her shoulder when it ached. From the beginning I was going to, unless there was a rule that you can't until the end.

CHAPTER THREE

I won't claim that I'm fearless or that I disdain to lie at any cost, but I will say that I don't bother to lie about every little thing. So when Edward asked me Sabbath morning after breakfast why I wasn't readying myself for Meeting, I didn't say I was sick; I said, "I'm not going. I'm expecting Sarah Dowling today."

I didn't know what time Sarah might come. It wasn't even certain that she had a way of telling time. I only knew that she didn't go to Meeting.

"Sarah Dowling?" Edward said.

Martha said, "That—that—" but her language was not equal to her thought. "Freak" is what she was groping for, I imagine. I allowed myself to feel a little flattered. If she slandered my friends, it could mean she liked me.

"She's a very fine person when you get to know her," I said. I wanted to say "lovely" too, but reconsidered.

"You shouldn't miss Meeting," Edward said. "It's not a light matter to miss Meeting."

That may sound like something said to impress children, but from Edward it was not. Even as a boy he was earnest and serious and afraid of being ill thought of. One time back in school, Edward's grade was studying Heaven, and since I always paid attention to all the other grades, I was listening from my smaller, more lowly seat.

27

"And there shall be no night there," the teacher said. Edward's grade, which means Edward and one other big boy, reacted with appropriate bafflement. "No *night?*" "No night," the teacher said, smiling conceitedly. And then Edward stood up and asked, all solemnly, "But won't there be a—period—of—lesser light?" I was so proud of him I could hardly contain myself. My big brother! Such wisdom! Such a question! So well put! The teacher said, "No. No. No indeed," but I could see that he was taking some credit for Edward too.

Well, that's just a little childhood memory, but it shows that Edward probably really meant it when he said it was no light matter to miss Meeting. I have always felt somehow responsible for Edward's taking religion so hard. Wasn't it in an effort to reach the untrembling hearts of the likes of me that the preacher laid it on so? If all faces had shown Edward's terror, wouldn't the preacher have been eager to reassure? Wouldn't he have said, "My children, my children, God means you no harm!"?

"She's not fit," Martha said, meaning Sarah.

I said, "She's very fit, a very fine young woman who happens to have the gumption to help her family. I honor her for it."

"There's fit ways and unfit ways," Martha said. She was so agitated she forgot she was sick and she took the children away from me and dressed them herself.

I didn't mind. It's trying to dress children, especially shoes. They deliberately hold their feet odd, and I don't feel they should be slapped just for that.

Edward was ready, dark-blue and white and stiff and dignified, standing by the fire. I went over to get some coals for my own fire.

I said, "She's coming to talk about our plans for going out to Genesee." I squatted down and heaped some coals together.

"That nonsense again?" he said, but he wasn't surprised

or even as gruff as he intended to be, so I knew he'd been thinking.

"Can you lend me a map of York State?"

"No sense in it."

"Please, Brother."

"What would folks think of me if I let you go off?"

I laughed. "They'd think it couldn't be so bad after all, if Edward White did it. Please lend me a map. Just for today."

He walked off. I felt the cold wind when he opened his parlor door. I had hopes for the map, but no certainty. Maybe he himself didn't know until he handed it to me that he was going to. Besides the map, he handed me a small book entitled *A Description of the Genesee Country, in the State of New York.*

"Edward!" I began, but then I could only smile.

"Don't carry these with coals," he said. "They're dear."

Sarah wore a dress. "Don't say nothing," she said. She would have looked all right in it except that it made her so miserable that she hung her head and scowled and stooped. She reminded me of a dog we'd clipped once to help him against the summer heat, and he hid until his coat grew back. I must admit we drove him to it by laughing at him. He did look so comical. And so did Sarah, but I had the memory of the dog to guide me and I pretended she looked just the same as always.

"I have a map of York State," I said. "I'm copying it for us. And wait till you see what else."

"Ma said it would look better for Sunday," Sarah said. "Listen to me!"

"I can't. I've got this cussed dress on."

Since I'd been waiting to laugh anyway, that set me off, and her too, not very happily at first but she warmed into it.

"Why, I just don't see how you stand it. My skirt's

all chunks of snow where it dragged. Like a sheep full of burrs. And where do you put your hands?"

"Here," I said, holding mine out to her. "Now that you're a woman I can treat you like one."

She looked at my hands and then at my face and then in confusion everywhere but at me, groping all the while for her breeches-top to hook her thumbs in.

I reached out and firmly took her hand. "Now," I said, "would you rather get warmed up or see the map or see the book? Everything at once, I think." I led her to the bench by the fire and then went over to the table where the treasures were. She began to pick snow pellets off the hem of her skirt and toss them slowly, one at a time, into the fire. They hissed and sputtered.

"There's several things to say," she said.

"Hundreds of things."

"I told Pa I'm going."

She stopped. To help her, I said, "I told Edward. He wants me to go. So much so that he feels duty-bound to stop me. He can't help feeling that anything that tempts him so much must be wrong. I suppose your father feels he can't spare you."

"Well, but he won't stop me. He can make another boy. The trouble is, when Rachel heard, she wanted to come too."

"Who's Rachel?" I shouted, and heard myself, and said again (fairly decently), "Who's Rachel?"

"My sister. You seen her."

"I saw dozens of identical girls. How should I know which one was Rachel?"

"She looks growed. Some of 'em don't." Sarah tossed a pellet into the fire. "She's set her heart on coming."

"You told her no."

"I told her I'd see."

"You told her *I'm* going?"

"I told her you was thinking on it."

"I have told you and told you and told you. How can

I be more definite?" I was being a little rough with the map, I noticed, so I took it back to the table. I stood there by the table trying to collect myself, looking at Sarah's back. She was bending to her hem again.

"What are you thinking?" I asked.

Still bent, she mumbled something. To hear, I moved over and stood behind her. She said, "Rachel's just like me. She never had things fine. She wouldn't fret."

"Would you leave me in this life I can't stand because I've had things fine?"

"This might be just play for you. You even said you might not stay."

"Did Rachel say she'd stay? Did she say, 'I'll stay, though I hate it and die of it!'? All right, I'll say that. I'll stay. Whatever happens."

"There's something else."

I groaned.

"There's what I feel," she said. "You might not like it."

"What do you feel?"

"I care for you."

"I want you to. I care for you."

"If it bothers you or anything I can stop. So tell me if you don't want me to."

"I don't want you to stop."

She straightened up and turned her head and looked up at me.

"Is it really all right?" she asked.

"Of course it's all right."

She leaned back against me then. "I think about you," she said. "Every day in the clearing I expect to see you again because I did once. That one time."

"I think about you, too," I said. I put my hands on her shoulders. She bent her left cheek down until it touched my hand.

"I keep thinking every shadow is you. Because when you came that day, there was this shadow in the corner of my eye that when I looked was you."

"I'll come often. And then we'll go together."

"I know it sounds like just talk, so soon, when I don't even know you yet." She pressed her lips against my hand. "I'd've waited, but I had to know what to tell Rachel." She kissed each knuckle and reached the edge of my hand and kissed it. I felt her waiting there for me to turn my palm up. I could feel her wish, and wondered why she couldn't feel mine, that she butt it up like a calf going for milk.

She shouldn't have been afraid. She should have felt my wish. To punish her, I said, "I'm wasting daylight, standing here."

She flung herself up. "Oh, *don't* waste *day*light! Where's my jerkin?" She rushed around blindly, looking for her jerkin. It was somewhere there. I myself couldn't see or remember.

"You didn't mean what I meant. It wasn't all right at all. Now what'll I do? Oh God, where's my jerkin?" She found it and thrust her arms into the sleeves. "Well, Miss White," she said, "you get on with your daylight and I'll get on——"

I stayed as she'd left me, looking down at the bench. I felt her gaze. She was trying by the strength of her wish to make me turn. I made her say it: "Won't you look at me?"

"Oh, wasn't I?" (My politest voice.) "I'm sorry. Are you leaving? Must you?"

"Oh, I can't go away without kissing you!"

And I felt her lips on my cheek, nibbling towards my mouth, and getting there, and staying; and I knew why she'd been afraid and wondered why I hadn't been, why I had lured this mighty mystery and astonishment into the room, into our lives.

I turned my head to save my life.

"Did I hold you too hard? Did I hurt you?"

"Oh, no!" I said. I pressed her even closer, to show.

"Was that a feeling I felt in you?"

I hesitated and then told true: "Yes."

She turned her face up, with the look of Jacob granted the Angel's blessing.

Her fear was over. Mine not. "That's something powerful, girl," I said.

She nodded, breathing through her mouth because she'd just come up from deep water. Then she looked down at me, all seriousness except a little turning-up of the right corner of her mouth. I looked back, seriously entirely, because it was up to me to save us from a thirst we could never come to a pause in or rest from. I was older. It was up to me.

She wouldn't look away. She wanted the corner of my mouth up too, and when at last I gave her that, she kissed me again.

Oh, we were begun. There would be no way out except through.

And that thought, that whatever this was I would live it, made it containable. I can't explain why. I only know it happened.

Once I'd dreamed that a fierce wildcat was attacking me. I was very afraid, and then I thought, why, it's hungry, and I offered it my hands to eat. It didn't eat them. It became immediately gentle, a friend.

So when I let my head fall back under Sarah's kiss, the frenzy I trembled at just wasn't there. Instead, comfort and joy and simplicity and order and answers to questions I'd always supposed unanswerable, such as, why was I born? why a woman? why here? why now?

A wonderful glowing spacious peacefulness came to us. There was so much time. I took her jerkin off and kissed it and laid it down. All afternoon we leaned against each other at the table, and in the light from the frosty window I read to her about Genesee—the price of salt (one dollar a bushel), the wages of a laborer (ten to fifteen dollars a month, and board), the number of republicans, the number of federalists. On and on, and then repeat. That the mail stage ran out from Albany twice a week. That unimproved land west of the Genesee River sold for a dollar and a half an acre.

"That's where we'll go, west of the river," Sarah said. "I'll cut my hair and be a laborer. We can buy near seven acres for a month of work." She couldn't read, but she could deal with figures in her head. I've always choked up at the thought of figures myself.

"We'll have other money, and you won't cut your hair," I said, very firmly, something like a man. I began to wonder if what makes men walk so lordlike and speak so masterfully is having the love of women. If that was it, Sarah and I would make lords of each other. Provided always that she didn't cut her hair.

At the end of the afternoon I bundled her up to go home, giving little kisses at every stage, and then more, and sent her off. Her face showed glory so bright I might have worried, except that I was sure no one else had any basis in experience for recognizing it, and I didn't think it would hold up through her long cold walk home anyway. Surely she'd get home red, frowning, and miserable like an ordinary person.

What Sarah wanted was to get aside by herself and imagine every detail about me, but a family that's spent a winter Sabbath crowded up in a country kitchen isn't likely to let a returned traveler hold back. They wanted news, and they'd learned to expect it from Sarah, who knew how to notice and remember. She always had some little thing to tell from going somewhere.

The little girls (her older sister was married and gone) tagged her up the ladder to the loft where she got out of her mother's dress and into her own breeches, and then back down again where she sat beside the fire and tried to dream. They were asking to be told, again, what my house was like, and what I was like, and whether I had jewels, and about Edward's children, and what color our dogs were, and how tall our woodpile. "No, no, I'm tired," she'd say, or, "I already told you that," laughing and trying to push them off. They were supposed to be knitting, or learning to.

She thought how pretty they were and that she loved them, and in the midst of being happy on this happiest of her days, she felt a completely unexpected grief because it was not certain that something wonderful would happen to them too. If she hadn't studied so long to be manly, she'd have wept. But all through, she stayed happy too.

Rachel was squatting beside the coals tending supper. She said nothing, asked nothing, but she kept looking up at Sarah's face.

"What's that burning?" Sarah's mother asked. "Why, you ninny, you've burnt the supper. Stayed right there by it and let it burn!"

It wasn't really burned, just beginning to be. The men (Sarah and her father) ate first. Sarah really didn't. She wasn't hungry, and then, unwisely, she remembered our kisses and her throat got big—it felt as big as a singing frog's—and she couldn't swallow.

Her father said, "Well, you've got yourself a nice job, waiting on that Patience White while she sets on a silken pillow. I expect you spent the day studying where to get a carriage for her to ride in. She'll ride out in a carriage and you'll walk out and meet her there."

Fathers, I think, are rather alike in the kinds of things they say when someone has a hope.

Sarah didn't answer. Couldn't, actually.

"Well, is that the plan?"

She shook her head and kept looking down.

"Oh, she's got to have a carriage. And you better figure on about a hundred pair of them silken slippers. They won't hold up long in the woods, and she couldn't wear no ordinary boots like no ordinary girl."

I suspect that a Chinese father would have said about the same, or English, or Esquimau.

Her father ate quickly, being spared Sarah's impediment—perhaps never having known it—and left the table. Then Sarah could leave it too.

She went directly to the loft and laid aside her clothes. She lay down on her cornhusk pallet and pulled the quilt over herself and folded her arms under her head and let loose the thought of me.

"With all that blue blood in her feet, she can't hardly," her father shouted, somewhere way off down there. He didn't interrupt Sarah's thoughts.

But Rachel climbed up. She interrupted. "Shove over," she whispered, and lay down on Sarah's pallet, though her own was right beside. She strained to see Sarah's face, but couldn't yet. Sarah could see very well, from having been in the dim light longer.

"What happened?" Rachel whispered. When Sarah said nothing, Rachel said, "Your face. It shows in your face. What happened?"

Sarah said, "I found my mate." She thinks she said that because it wouldn't have been fair to let it seem that Rachel had to stay behind for an unimportant reason. I think she just plain wanted to tell.

"Who?" Rachel asked, alarmed but not forgetting to whisper.

"Patience White."

"And she goes with you and I stay here?"

"Fraid so, Sister."

Rachel pressed her face against Sarah and wept. Sarah held her, whispering, "Never mind, Sister. Pretty soon the one for you will come, and you'll be glad you're not out there with me. You'll be glad about your whole life."

"I hate her. She's rich and that's why."

"No. I love her. I love her."

"It's always been you and me." Rachel lifted herself and looked at Sarah. "From the start. When the babies was inside Ma and she couldn't get up and feed us or anything. When they was coming and we was scared she was dying, wasn't it always you and me holding together? Before we could talk plain we held together. How can you say you love somebody but me?"

"It's different. She kissed me. I never felt such a feeling."

"I'll kiss you." Rachel pushed her dry frightened lips against Sarah's. "You want something else? I'll do that too. More'n *she* ever would."

"Oh, Sister, don't. The one for you will come. Man or woman."

Rachel sat up and dried her tears and nose on her sleeve. They kept filling and she kept drying them. Sarah watched her, not knowing anything to say or do. In time the tears stopped.

"I wouldn't have nobody but a man," Rachel said.

"If it happens that way to you. It happened this way to me, and I'm really happy."

"I used to worry about you. That no man would have you. I never thought to worry you'd think you *was* a man."

"I'm not. I'm a woman that's found my mate."

"Oh, shut up!"

So Sarah rolled over. Rachel sat a while before climbing down.

In a house so small the only solitude anyone had was that given by a turned back.

Sarah fell asleep easily.

CHAPTER FOUR

Monday when I woke I thought first thing of Sarah. Instantly my bosom filled, as though with milk, and tingled. I lay there thinking how fine it was to be a woman and have a part that could please me the way my bosom did from just a thought, and imagining Sarah, waking now too, thinking of me and glad to be a woman.

How easy it was to wake that morning, when the world and my life in it were for the first time more interesting and beautiful than any dream I could lose by waking. So many times I had wished to be like a bear and not get up till spring, but that morning the cold couldn't touch me, and I would not have been a bear and foregone a winter's kisses for anything in earth or heaven.

There had been more snow during the night, and a wind to blow the paths full. Tobe was shoveling towards the barn when I went out to do my milking. "Well, you sure look happy," he said. He smiled, tobacco brown.

"I am—I am," I said and stepped into the snow he hadn't got to yet. He'd been shoveling for a fair while, though, and he'd chopped a hole in the creek to let the cattle drink. A small limping lonely old man, Tobe. How did he get up in the morning? Had anything beautiful happened to him his whole life long? How could he smile when he saw me happy? His pleasure in my pleasure seemed a generosity so unlikely as to make me think, at first, that he must have changed. Then I saw, of course, that I myself had, and I felt a pang at how many years I'd wasted not knowing that kindness was everywhere around, common as stone; and I felt also another gratitude to Sarah, for fixing me so I'd know from then on.

My two cows, as always when I entered the barn, began at once to sigh and drip milk. I find that so interesting. Martha's cows always did that too, at the sight of her but not of me. Martha considered it a waste, and I suppose it was, especially in winter, but how interesting.

There is something very dear and good about cows. They are gentle, alert, calm, and fresh-smelling. I put their careful winter portions into their mangers, and while they fed I pressed my brow hard against their warm, gurgling, dingy flanks, seized the flabby tits, and drew out the scanty thin winter milk. "Dear friend," I murmured, "Sarah and you and your cow friend and I are going to where you'll be slick and bountiful and the streets are paved with kisses."

I knew of course that for some years the cows couldn't have even a barn, and that when they did get one it wouldn't compare with this, my father's pride. Sarah's and mine would be of logs and small. My father's barn was fine, all boards and huge pegged beams and stone. It had a vast crammed hayloft, which was why we could milk all winter, and a threshing floor, and bins for grain, and many stalls, and cover for the plows and other tools, and cover for the buggy and sleigh. It had a special place for breaking and hatcheling flax, something we didn't do any longer of course, and a root cellar, and, as a last detail, in the stone of the retaining wall beside the stable door, a gap, a cave-mouth, leading into a cozy little lair for dogs. The dogs would never play in it, and even though my father had felt only playful when he built it, once he had it made he wanted it used and he was angry and puzzled at the dogs. I was a child then, and wanted the dogs to keep house as much as my father did, so I was angry and puzzled too. One day I put my head inside the dog-cave, and heard a sound like a distant waterfall or a conch shell held to the ear, and I think that faint roaring is the reason the dogs were so ungrateful. My father said nonsense, and my brother said nonsense, but I still think that was the reason.

So I whispered enticing lies to my cows and enjoyed their sturdy warmth. Since Martha didn't come out to do her milking, I went on and did it for her. I used to feel that I did her milking more often than not, but I must not have really, since her cows didn't drip for me and did for her.

When I took her milk to her, she was embarrassed but, if I may say so, I was very pleasant. "I was glad to do it," I said, and smiled, and asked if there was any other way I might help her.

"No, I'm managing. Edward says we'll be losing you."

"Yes, if you want to call it a loss."

"I might just begin to."

"I can see now where I could have done better."

"I can see where you wouldn't take the interest you would for your own," she said.

I thought it better not to explain that it was a different need unsatisfied that left me grudging. I wanted to, and I wanted to say I thought I understood how she could go down into the valley of pain and shadows and fear every year for Edward and his babies, now that I had found someone I would do that for if need be. Nothing I wanted to say seemed advisable, so I just gave Martha a hug and smiled and went to my place and set myself to copying the map of York State.

Around noon, Edward came to see me. He looked much as usual, very stern. He stomped around. My longing to tell my good news was a trial. To him I wanted to say, oh, Edward, I know where to get the joy that makes it easy to go on living: from *kisses*, Edward! But I'd

learned at age four, from his shock when I tried to teach
him how to get a wonderful feeling inside by moving in
a certain way, that there are things one doesn't tell Edward. So instead of recommending kisses for getting the
heaviness out of his step and the downward trend out of
his mouth, I smiled and said, "Good morning, Brother."

He said, "No, not very good. Sarah Dowling's making
it her brag that you're her mate."

And after all my longing to make that brag myself, I
felt my head burn in the mightiest blush of my life. My
throat clamped shut and saved me from speaking while I
waited for my surprise and dread to pass. The surprise did
pass. I saw that I should have known Sarah would tell,
being as tempted as I was, and innocent, and the most
honest person in the world. But the dread remained and
filled my mouth with dust. I seemed to hear all the
neighbors, and all the village, wondering and mocking
and scandalized, and my life made an example of. Out-
cast, I thought, and shut my teeth to bite back a groan.

"Well?" Edward said.

So I saw there was still a chance, at least with him. He
was ready to consider that there had been a misunder-
standing. Dear judicious Edward. I had no intention of
testifying against myself. Our Constitution says we needn't.
But what would it profit Sarah and me to persuade Edward, if the village had heard or would hear?

Nevertheless I had to try. We needed Edward's help in
order to leave.

I succeeded in saying, "Partner, she must mean."

"No, something like wife she means."

I produced a tiny astonished laugh, in the hope of mis-
leading him without having to tell an outright lie. "She
couldn't mean that. Who ever heard of such a thing?"

"She's bragging it. Her Pa was just here. Pretty riled up.
And I don't blame him. He wanted to see you. I said
I'd take care of it."

"Take care of what? I'd be very glad to see him. And

Sarah. To ask her what she could be thinking of. I think I'd better. Don't you, really?"

"I wouldn't advise it. He said to keep you off his place. I said I would."

"I'm just bewildered. What could she be thinking of?"

"She says the two of you are like man and woman."

"It's so impossible."

"If it's not so, I'm glad to hear it."

"How could it be so?" Then I had another question, and I very much feared the answer to it: "Who's she telling such things?"

His answer left me still in dread, uncertain. "She told her folks. I don't know who else. I don't expect her folks will brag on it. I sure won't. You just go on about your business and see no more of any of them, and maybe that'll be an end to it."

I said, "I expect that would be best," which was not at all the same as saying I would do it.

"That's better sense than I thought you had," he said. "You just govern yourself better in the future and we'll say no more."

I nodded one embarrassed nod, like a handshake sealing a bargain.

"I'll take these," he said, rolling up his map and gathering in his book. I didn't protest. I had the main part of the map copied off anyway, and Sarah and I had most of the book set to memory. He started to leave.

"Edward?"

"Yes?"

"Don't tell Martha?"

"I don't tend to tell Martha much."

Having been so evasive myself, I couldn't fail to notice that he didn't say he wouldn't.

Sarah was chopping in her clearing that morning, throwing all her muscle in, feeling wonderful. Her father came up behind her and stopped her ax by catching its handle, and took it from her. That was one of his tricks, not surprising except that she hadn't heard him coming.

She felt more than mellow, so she grinned at him. He liked to be grinned at, man to man, when he did something like that. She was too happy to notice that he was in a rage.

She even had some grin left when he said, "I've just come from seeing Edward White."

She waited. There were so many reasons for seeing Edward White. But she blushed.

"About your carryings-on," he said.

"What carryings-on?"

"It's too late to play sly. Rachel told me all about it."

Sarah's thought must have been as crystal-clear as usual, because he then said, "And you don't wallop her for it! I'll see to that."

He held the ax while he talked. It looked so small and light in his big hairy hands.

"Me and Edward White agreed to put a stop. He'll keep his gal to home, and I'll keep you." He held out the ax to her. "Get back to work now. I just figured you ought to know you won't be seeing her."

She ignored the ax. "I will be," she said, setting off. Long stubborn strides, too proud to run. He was forty-two, at the height of his strength but past his speed. He might not have caught her if she'd run. As it was, he had it easy.

He caught her and turned her around and slapped her several times—five times, she thinks—across the face. She felt no pain, only surprise; he hadn't struck her since the natural educating blows of childhood, such as to teach her not to crawl into the fire, and she had come to believe that he wouldn't. He wasn't generally a mean man. He was too big to need to be. He liked to taunt and bellow and lay down the law, but nobody had cause to be afraid of him.

She can't remember where her hands were or why they

weren't fighting him. Not that she could have prevailed
against his great toughness and strength, but she could
have tried. Something about hitting one's father, perhaps.

Then he let go of her jerkin with a push. She stumbled
backwards and fell. While she was lying there, propped
on one elbow, feeling her face and looking at him with
a rage as huge as his, he said, "That's to show, if you
don't know enough to do right, I can still make you. Who
do you think they'd blame if this got out? With all the
trouble I've got in this churchy place, you want to let that
holy bitch climb onto you again!"

He turned his back and went his way. She didn't chase
him with the ax or anything. She just stayed there in the
snow, studying how to get past him and down the road
and then past Edward, and, after all that, what kind of a
welcome she'd get from me.

My anxiety came and went all afternoon, like one of
Martha's long labors alternating pain and rest. For several
minutes I'd be calm, plotting how to save Sarah and me,
and then, like a labor pain, the bottom would fall out of
my heart and my tongue would go clitchy and my throat
like a stone. I would pace the floor and wring my hands
and regret that I'd ever clapped eyes on Sarah. Like a bird
with only one song, I'd say, "Betrayed! Betrayed!" and
think of myself as like Jesus and Sarah as Judas, and
then, more moderately, as Peter. Foolish and impetuous
and weak, like Peter.

At one point I even tried to make a picture, since
picture-making was a tested way of expressing and calm-
ing myself. My hands were too unsteady and I had to give
it up. It was to be Jesus kneeling at prayer, and Peter with
a group of British redcoats shaking his head (he was to
have two faces, to show the shake) while the cock
stretches himself up and utters a long bright wiggle.

During a calm period, I went out to do my evening
milking. Tobe was in the yard. It seemed to me that he

looked at me knowingly, as though he'd overheard Sarah's father. "So that's what's made you happy, happy missy!" I heard him think. I wanted to say, "No, I never loved her, no I never kissed her, no I'm not her mate," and I knew then which of us was Peter, and how Peter felt, and what made him deny the only light he'd ever known.

I hurried past Tobe, with my face turned away, despising my Peter nature but bound in it. While milking, I decided not to be Peter. I decided to be brave and upright like Sarah, but when I started back to the house with the milk, another cramp of cowardice hit me and I crossed the yard like a spy.

My kitchen felt like a haven. I began to spin. The wheel squeaked and whirred and the filaments of wool turned to yarn between my fingers. I spun like a spinning machine. Suppertime came. I didn't feel like eating so I spun right through. Night blacked my window. I lit no lamp. The firelight served.

I was waiting for Sarah to come and tell me how it happened and teach me how not to be Peter, but she didn't come. My eyes burned from lack of juice and needed closing. At around midnight, remembering for the first time her dogs and ours, I lowered my winter-bed and climbed into it. Hours passed and I was still awake, picturing how Sarah tried to climb down from her upper window and set her dogs to howling. Dogs will howl over the most familiar thing if they judge it out of place. And Sarah was out of place clinging to a house wall at night. I couldn't stop seeing. She wouldn't come. I couldn't sleep.

How would I do my next day's work without sleep, I worried, and then I thought, why, I'll be sick, like any other woman. I laughed a little and fell asleep.

CHAPTER FIVE

Not knowing how far our tale had traveled, I was careful with everyone, not to act differently, not to be odd. I concentrated and moved everywhere as though watched.

At family prayers, Edward asked God to guide me to the realization that we are not born to be happy but to do our duty and to save our souls. Tobe and Martha seemed to think just my laziness was meant.

Sabbath at Meeting and after, I was alert to any change in feeling toward me. I listened for a rustle when I walked in, watched for any hint that I was of particular interest. I found none. Slowly I began to feel safe.

And the moment I felt safe, I longed for Sarah's kiss. I had not been able to wish for it until then.

I made a plan, but it was one Sarah alone would have to carry out, and its success depended on nobody's knowing that I had recommended it. We had to seem not to have had a chance to consult. So I waited. I seemed to surrender, but I was waiting, patiently, like a cat that knows it can win if it waits, even though it's not strong enough to break open the mouse's nest. Sarah, incapable of guile, would never think of a plan; but my chance would come to tell her mine. Someone's vigilance would lapse. An ally would appear. Something would happen in our favor, and when it did I would be ready.

She couldn't, of course, know that. Even as I couldn't know that every day she was boldly and heroically and stupidly setting off on the road to my house, and being caught and beaten by her father. She would not beg or explain or discuss. She knew that if she lived, she would get to me. What he did was up to him. Her choice was fixed. No one but me could tell her to stay away from me.

It is a sin to raise a girl to be a man, believing in strength and courage and candor. We can't prevail that way. Of course her father caught her and beat her and dragged her back. She knew he would, but she counted on his finally tiring, and having other interests. Before that happened, she could be a ruin.

There'd be that huge man pounding her, and Rachel wailing, "Pa! Pa! Don't!" and all the little girls wailing too and the mother silent night and day. He came to hate Sarah, I think, for making him be a bully when he wasn't one at heart, and making all his family silent at the sight of him where there'd been love before. And he couldn't even explain. If he could have explained, they would have supported him. They thought (except Rachel) that he only wanted to keep Sarah forever and make her work for him. Maddening to be thought cruel, when you're guided by nothing but the loftiest moral purpose.

Then Sarah would get up and slowly go back into her house, the way to mine being furiously barred, shaking off Rachel's efforts to support and guide and comfort her. Slowly she'd climb up to her pallet. It was the end of clearing the new field for that winter.

"Sister, Sister, *quit*. He won't *let* you!" Rachel whispered. She'd followed Sarah up.

Sarah looked at her and then tried to turn away but couldn't, being lame. So she shut her eyes dismissingly.

"I can't stand this every day," Rachel said. It had been then ten days.

"Pa'll get so he can't either," Sarah said. "I don't feel it at the time."

This was the first Sarah had spoken to her in the whole ten days, so Rachel was able to fetch snow for Sarah's bruises. She carried the snow in a pan past her father, who was sulking by the fire and who said not a word.

Then opening Sarah's clothes, finding bruises (how not find them?), holding snow against them, Rachel murmured, "Bullhead, do you have to just put your horns down and run blind? He don't want to hurt you. He don't even want to keep you. He just wants an excuse now to stop. Can't you see he's just pleading with you to tell him a lie, so he can stop pounding you?"

"I haven't got one," Sarah said.

And then Rachel produced the selfsame plan I'd made myself, showing that female minds run in the same channel.

"You just say it was all a lie, what you said before," Rachel said.

"But it wasn't."

"*Say* so. Say here's your chance to get to the West where the men all are, at the expense of this well-to-do lady that wants the same but's too scared to go alone."

"I already said I love her. Didn't you tell him that?"

"Well, *now* you say you didn't think how that would sound. You thought it sounded better than being greedy for her money. But now you see the truth would've been better."

Sarah had never dreamed women could be so sly. "I won't say that against my feeling," she said and shut her eyes and soul and pushed the pan of snow away.

Then, on second thought, she looked at Rachel again and asked, "Why did you tell him?"

With tears, Rachel said, "I didn't know he'd take on so. I thought maybe it was a common thing. We never know what's common, living back here like this. I was worried and I thought maybe he'd say it was nothing to worry about. I never knew he'd take on so."

And even with an example of Rachel's slyness so fresh in her mind, Sarah believed her.

I'm not proud of myself for this next part, but I'm proud of Sarah, and I have to tell mine to tell hers.

Sarah was at my door. I gasped at the sight of her, and took her arm to draw her in. Her eyes were bruised, face puffy, lip swollen and split, eyebrow cut. "Pa's here," she said, and, yes, he was, leaning against the wall beside the door. I hadn't noticed anything except the condition of Sarah's face, but when I saw him hulking there my heart began to pound so loud I thought it would deafen me and maybe deafen them too.

They both came in. I shut the door and leaned against it. I was very afraid. We were all mute. Soon I felt the door move, and Edward came in. I suppose Tobe or the children had seen them come and told him. I didn't care. I may even have been a little glad. Sarah and I were lost anyway. At least Edward could talk.

"Was that necessary, Dowling?" he asked, tilting towards Sarah's damages.

"I didn't really hurt her. Just bare hands. That cut there's the only one she's got. Her own bone did that."

Edward's lips made an excellent scornful line. "Well, what brings you?"

"She was set on it. I thought there'd be no harm as long as I came too. Speak up, gal. We won't stay long."

She glanced at them, waiting for them to stand back and let us talk, but they stood right there, wouldn't budge, and she looked at me and braced herself and said, "Do you still want to go?" She looked at me with love, right there in front of them. I felt angry at her. Embarrassed.

"We can't," I said, because we couldn't unless Edward bought me out and Sarah's father stopped guarding her. We'd need so much help to go, and they'd set their wills against our going, and it was hopeless, and I couldn't remember love. It was far away and lost, like infancy, and a mistake anyway.

"We can, unless you don't want to."

"It wasn't very reasonable," I said.

Her father said, "There, Sal, you've got your answer. Now let's go."

"If you want to, we'll find a way," she said.

"There is no way," I said.

"You've got your answer. You was played with," her father said. "Now come on."

She said, "Do you *want* to?"

As a pauper and a fugitive? For a love I couldn't remember the feel of? I didn't want to. I wasn't strong enough. I had to know what I was strong enough for. I had to know that much.

"No."

With a great wailing groan she made for the door.

I let her go. There was no more to say. Then when she and her father were out the door, there was one more thing to say.

"Sarah!" I called. She faced me so fast, so hopeful.

"Don't you care what people think?"

"Course I care," she said. She turned away. She stumbled as she walked away. I shut the door.

Edward was still with me. For something to do, not to look at him or talk, I sat down to spin. He was standing in the middle of my kitchen, just standing there, for the longest time. Go, go, go, go, go, I thought. Out, Edward.

"She really feels," he said, slowly. "I never knew anybody to feel so much. Not even a man."

I faced again my fate as spinster sister and aunt, but it was worse now because I believed it, as I never really had before. I knew myself unable to change my life.

I worked at forgetting what I thought I knew when Sarah kissed me. That whole day came to seem very childish and foolish and unworthy of me. I struggled for calm and unselfishness, to be of service to others, and I thought, why, this is suffering, this is the pain of life, this is what they talk about in Church, this daily struggle to keep going without knowing why. And I saw what was meant by faith: faith is the belief that this life is not our only chance. Wavering of faith means beginning to believe in this life and wanting to live it, denying all duties and dashing off uncontrolled. What would I do, I wondered, all uncontrolled and raging and self-seeking, my tiger-soul unchained, these dangerous passions freed? I would seek Sarah's lips again and be calm.

The story of the Prodigal Son attracted and warned me. He demanded his patrimony, as I had meant to demand mine. He squandered it. I tried to imagine how one might squander—what dissolute living might consist in. Searching my soul for an answer, I found again my longing for Sarah's lips. But that wasn't dissolute in a man. Men could have women's lips. And I felt, I think for the first time, a rage against men. Not because they could say, "I'm going," and go. Not because they could go to college and become lawyers or preachers while women could be only drudge or ornament but nothing between. Not because they could be parents at no cost to their bodies. But because when they love a woman they may be with her, and all society will protect their possession of her.

BOOK TWO

Sarah

CHAPTER ONE

Pa and me walked home, single file, him first. The tears just poured down my face. I couldn't've stopped them even if he'd been looking.

I'd made the mistake of letting a feeling get past the point where it can be stopped. You can't stop tears if they get as far as your eyes, or even to your throat. Only place to stop them is in the feeling, keeping it out. But I didn't see, and still don't, how I could've done different —not felt for Patience. And once I'd felt, I had to stand whatever happened.

Pa said, half over his shoulder, "I see now I wouldn't't've had to lay it on so."

I didn't answer.

"No hard feeling?" he asked.

"No, Pa."

And I really didn't have a grudge against him. I knew that if Patience had felt what I did, nothing Pa did could've kept her from me. I knew that by his own lights, Pa'd acted right. I couldn't hold that against him. And I didn't. I was just finished with him.

We walked along. I could feel every place he'd hit me. I hadn't much before. But then I could.

"I'll be leaving, soon's I heal up," I said.

"Like you was planning." He nodded, like broad-minded. "Now, *that's* all right."

I was really finished with him. I didn't even hackle up and ask what made him think it mattered to have him say it was all right.

"I think you'll be back," he said.

"No."

"I think so. But I think you need to find that out for yourself. And that's all right. When you want to come back, I just want you to know you've got a place."

I would hang myself by the neck before I would come back, but I didn't say so. I just walked along behind him.

I clumb up to my bed soon's I got home. Rachel came at me right away. I had no grudge against her either, but I could see that I was through with her too. I knew she never meant to harm me. It didn't matter. It was like an ax had come down and cut me from her. I wondered if that was how Patience felt about me.

Rachel said, "Oh, Sister, where you been? What happened?"

I just shook my head and turned away.

All I wanted was to heal up and get out of there.

I didn't go down for supper. Pa yelled for me. I thought next he'd send up one of the little ones, knowing I still had feeling for them. I braced myself. I'd say, gentle, no, I wasn't hungry.

But it was Ma that came. She shouldn't've! With her lame shoulder, up the ladder like that, with her shoulder like that—"Oh, Ma!"

"Now, gal," she said.

"I just want to heal up and go."

"Sure. I always knew you'd go."

"Patience don't want to."

"She's scared."

"Scared? You think so? She didn't say so. She just said, no, she didn't want to."

"She's too scared to think if she wants to."

All the while, Ma was wiping my eyes and nose on her skirt. Hard-woven linsey, scratchy. It shouldn't've felt so comfortable. It took me back to when I could reach no higher than her skirt. Oh what a skirt she's had through the years, smeared with baby noses.

I said, "She won't come."

"No, she won't."

"I can't stay here."

"No, you can't."

By March I was healed up. Every outside part of me worked just right. There wasn't a bruise to show. I didn't cry for Patience except when nobody could see.

I cut my hair. The family talked against it, but nobody stopped me. They stood around and watched, like watching a fist fight but not getting into it.

We had no looking glass. I just felt and cut. My head felt light and strange and cool and free. It would take some getting used to. When I'd got to where I couldn't catch any more locks, I stopped.

Ma said, "I'll even it up for you." I felt the blades cold on my neck. Everybody allowed it was uncanny how like a boy I looked when she got through.

I didn't know what I'd do when my hair needed another cut. Patience was supposed to bring shears.

"You know there's a toll for walking down a turnpike?" Pa said.

I didn't know. For just walking?

"I won't walk down a turnpike, then," I said.

"There's a toll for bridges," he said. "And ferryboats."

"I'll swim."

I figured I could walk fifteen miles a day, at least, and work here and there as I went for my eats. Ma'd fed many a man on his way like I'd be. I knew it could be done and was done. They'd been by our fire and told, and made me want to go. I don't know why they didn't make Pa want to. How could he stay in Connecticut on that rocky hilly farm that had been butchered before we ever laid eyes on it, and not feel his heart just break to go? The only way I can explain Pa on that is to say he never had that hopefulness you need to push out and try. He might look big and cheery and reckless, but inside he's very scared to take a chance.

There was no use starting till the mud dried out and let the farmers at their fields so they'd be glad to swap a meal for a little help. I was fit to go, but I waited around, teaching my sister Mary how to use an ax and drive the cattle. Pa skipped Rachel—he figured she was past the age. I wanted to teach Mary how to handle a gun too, but Pa said that was going too far. He wished he'd never taught me, he said. Mary was going to help him, but she wasn't going to get big ideas about herself. He'd learned his lesson, he said. I have to laugh at Pa thinking it's having a big idea to do like him. "I don't want Mary claiming her name's Mark one of these days," Pa said.

My new name was Sam. Did learning to shoot cause that? I expect it could've. It made me feel I could take care of myself, and not be beholden, and love who my feeling went to. I suppose lots of girls loved Patience but never said. Maybe it was because I could shoot that I could say. No matter that Patience changed her mind and I had to cry and go alone. I was never for a minute sorry I'd said.

Came the day I left home, a Monday late in April. I was up early and everybody with me. I hoped the little ones would sleep on, but they got up, crying. I was crying too, but that had nothing to do with how I had to go.

I laid my blanket on the floor and put my extra clothes and tinderbox along it, and the jag of nocake and jerky Ma had for me, and then I rolled the blanket long, like a log, and bent it and tied the ends together so I could hang it around my neck and over one shoulder. It rode easy that way. Pa let me take a hatchet, on grounds I'd be back before he could miss it, and I hung that at my waist, along with a little pan Ma gave me, and I was ready to go except I didn't know how to.

Ma kissed me and said, "I wish we had some money for you."

"I'll make my way," I said.

"I know. You'll be just fine."

"Ma, I'll come back if you need me. Just let me know."

She nodded, playing there would be a way she could let me know, and said, "Now, off you go."

Pa said, "You won't get twenty mile."

I kissed them all. Even Pa. "I won't say goodbye," he said. "You'll be back in two days."

"Off you go," Ma said.

"Don't tell *no*body you're a girl," Pa said. "Nobody! Hear?"

I set off. I hardly could, but just by taking one step and then the next, I did it.

But I couldn't get up any enthusiasm, and I knew I had to try Patience one more time, to make sure. It wouldn't make sense to get all the way to Genesee and *then* wonder what she'd say if I asked her again.

And no matter what she said, maybe she'd give me one last kiss.

So I cut back and around through the woods to Patience's place, and stood, scared, in the road looking at her house all grand and white, and me with everything I owned across my shoulder and not heavy. I could see how there was never any real reason to expect anything.

But I'd come out of my way to make sure, and after the racket her dogs made I knew I must've been seen. I went on up and thumped the main front door. The door to Patience's part was inside, down the hall, but I couldn't very well go in there after all that had been.

Who came to the door was Mrs. White, Edward White's wife, the one that wouldn't let me warm up the day I fetched the wood. She didn't know me as a boy. She was almost pleasant at first, but soon's I said who I was she shut the door all but a crack, like I was dangerous, and peeked out at me. I felt the air on my head and wished for my hair back. I felt my plaguy face and ears get red. No way to stop them. The blood just went. I stood still and played I didn't notice.

"I came to see Patience, Miss White," I said.

"She's gone."

"Gone! Where?"

"Visiting."

"Oh."

She wanted to shut the door then, so even though I was choking I had to hurry to say, "Tell her I came by. Tell her I'm heading out. Tell her I said goodbye."

Then I could go. Going couldn't be fast enough or hard enough to suit me. I wanted to walk till my feet bled and my knuckles dragged and my belly broke, to see if maybe I could hurt enough someplace else to tire out the knot in my chest.

CHAPTER TWO

My road ran first northwest and then veered northeast, up the valley of the Hooestennuc River, the way the men who stopped at our place talked about. Even at flood from spring runoff, the river showed its biggest rocks. The rest of the year it showed the smallest too. You couldn't take a boat up it, or ship to market on it, but it did give me many a drink, and it marked the easiest grade through a tangly batch of steep hills.

I planned to rest often and be sensible, so my strength would hold through the many weeks I'd be walking. But on that first day, every time I stretched out in the roadside grass I got so jumpy I had to set right off again. I had to put space between me and all I was lonesome for— Ma and Mary and the little ones, and Patience. I kept thinking Patience could be home again by now, and I should ask her again. It was a dangerous thought, that made me weak. I wouldn't be able to trust myself until I'd gone too far, so far I couldn't turn back.

To save my boots, I carried them, tied together, over my shoulder. I settled into a good ground-covering swing. A man can walk four miles an hour, but I don't think I was making that much. All Connecticut tilts up to the north, to let the rivers run down to the Sound, so even where I seemed to have a flat way I knew I was going

uphill. It would be uphill all the way. All to the good,
I thought. It would help my belly break.

But my hip joints worked so smooth, and my muscles
felt so long and strong, that I kind of knew I wasn't about
to break. I kind of didn't want to break, anyway. My feet
had soles like boot leather, and arches like stone bridges.
They wouldn't bleed. They'd carry me to the edge of
the world if I wanted to go that far. Just up Connecticut
and Massachusetts and across York State would be easy.

Noontime I knew I had to eat. I didn't want to stop
already, while somebody might still say, "Why, you ain't
Sam *No*body, you're Ira Dowling's gal." I went until I
crossed a creek, and stopped then and unrolled my blanket
and ate, very slow, in little bits, a little jerky and a little
nocake, with a whole lot of water between bits.

Then on again, covering ground. It was a pretty day,
April and all. Just right.

Towards night I asked a farmer could I sleep in his
barn. He looked me over for something to be against, but
there I was, a simple farmer boy. "Reckon," he said, so
I went on into his haymow, which was pretty much empty,
as could be expected by April. There was a little hay,
though—folks do hate to feed the last of it till they see
the next will be along—and I scooped what I could into
a nest and flopped down.

The farmer came in and perched on the edge of the
mow and pecked away at me with questions. I told everything true except my name. He said I'd never get to
Genesee. He said I was a fool and should've stayed where
I was. He said I was no twenty-one, without a whisker
like I was, and shouldn't claim it.

I asked if he had a chore or two I might do for some
supper. He said he figured he could spare me a little
samp and milk, being as it looked like a good year, and
being as he had a boy himself, older though, pushing
out through that godforsaken wilderness somewhere.
Never mind the chores.

I hope his boy fared better than the summer did. It was the famous summer of 1816 when it snowed off and on over most of New England the whole summer long. But it still looked all right in April.

I ate with his family. There were some girls, and then a boy only sixteen with some sure-enough sprouts on his chin. He wanted to hear all about Genesee. I told him all I could, in my deepest voice. The girls listened too, one in particular.

My eyes kept closing by themselves, but the boy wouldn't stop asking me what it was like out there. He followed me out to the barn, asking, and was still asking when I fell asleep.

Someone's touch made me stir. I thought it was the boy, and mumbled, "I told you all I know." I thought it was still night and I hadn't slept at all, but it was earliest morning, dawn, with the birds really blaring, and who woke me was the girl who'd listened so.

"Sam, you have to go," she said. "Now. Hurry."

I woke right up and started rolling my pack before I asked, "Why?"

"Papa's going to turn you in as a runaway prentice."

"But I ain't."

"I don't know. I just know he's going to, for the reward. He said last night. I let you sleep till birdsong."

I stepped down behind the barn. I guess she didn't peek, because she still called me "Sam" when I went back in to get my pack. She had cheese and a big cut of bread for me, and some milk that I drank right away so's to leave her the cup.

She kept looking at me peculiar and standing peculiar, sort of close to me. I didn't know what to make of her.

"I'm obliged to you," I said, if that was what she wanted.

"It's nothing." She kept on.

"I better get off," I said.

She said, "You better," but she had me by the arm and I didn't like to jerk away.

"It's getting pretty light. They'll be about," I said.

And she pushed up and kissed me.

I was just so surprised. Did girls act like that with boys as a regular thing?

Before I had a chance to enjoy the kiss it was over and she was laughing and pushing me out saying, "Good luck, Sam. You're sweet. Hurry."

Just remembering her kiss kept me grinning and I stepped along so fine. Being a boy was going to be pretty good. I pictured girls all the way to Genesee giving me little laughy kisses and keeping my spirit up. I began to see it might be better this way than getting all tore up by caring a lot. A kiss that you feel deep tears you deep later when it's lost. But a laughy kiss hurries you on your way and makes the miles fly.

People I passed looked at me and I felt so good I smiled even when they didn't. We're not strong for smiling in Connecticut, as a rule. I didn't take it personal.

Towards night, again, I asked to be put up. The farmer this time made me work for it, mending a stone wall the winter had thrown down. I was near spoiled enough to think I shouldn't have to. Then his wife fed me good and gave me the use of a husk mattress. I threw it down on the floor of the empty corncrib and slept like on a cloud.

Next morning I couldn't get out. I pounded and hollered, and was just starting with my hatchet when the farmer came up.

"Don't do that, boy," he said.

"Well, let me out then."

"We'll just wait a while."

"What for?"

"For the newspaper," he said. "To see who's looking for a runaway prentice about five foot eight with brown hair that likes to say he's twenty-one but he's no more'n fourteen, and whatever his name is it ain't Sam. Leastwise if you say, 'Sam,' he half the time don't hear."

"I'm no prentice."

"If they's nothing in the paper, I'll let you go and no harm done."

"I got a long ways to go. You let me out or I'll chop my way out."

"You chop my corncrib, boy, and the sheriff will see to you."

I believed him, and I didn't have time for sheriffs.

"When's the paper come?"

"Any day now it should be along."

"Any day!"

"Just settle in."

His wife pushed my eats between the slats. I studied what would make her help me, like turn her back and close her ears while I broke out. Her face was so mean and tired I doubted anything would.

I'm ashamed to say I let him keep me two days, even though I could've pried my way out easy while they slept. I didn't quite want to sleep on the bare ground with snakes about. Snakes have always been a little hard for me. Pa used to say I was a pretty fair boy except about snakes. I'd worked my feelings around to where I could face them all right awake, but I didn't like the idea of being asleep around them.

So I let that farmer waste two days for me before the paper came and he turned me loose. He still thought I was a prentice and that the next paper would say so, but he kept his word and let me go.

I pushed on. I could see where it might take a good long time to get to Genesee.

My next farmer said right off, "A runaway prentice!" but he thought I was just right to run away and not be ground down and abused. "He didn't feed you right, did he? He didn't clothe you warm. He didn't teach you nothing. Come on, Sam, you can tell me."

"But I'm no prentice."

"Sam, I'm your friend. I'm *for* you. I wouldn't turn you in. I know them wicked masters. Just cause you're big for your age, they work you like an ox. How old are you, Sam? Fourteen?"

I suppose I should've thought up a tale for him, he wanted one so.

Well, that's how it went. I pushed clear to Massachusetts without finding anyone that didn't hold me back one way or the other—to get a reward for me, or try to draw a tale out of me—and I got no more kisses. I began to see how boys aren't much better off than women. Men are the ones who get their way and run the world. I began to see that I could stop looking like a boy in ten or twenty more years without looking any more like a man, and that even if I could fight past all these people and get to Genesee, I still wouldn't be paid a man's wages or let to make my way.

If it hadn't been that Pa was expecting me, I might've gone back.

I was that discouraged.

But no matter how I felt, I kept the sun at my back and the river at my haw side, and kept on. There'd be wagons on the road, and some buggies, and folks would slow down to look me over, but nobody offered to carry me, and I took care not to look interested in being carried. I'd stopped looking for help from folks. I got so I didn't even look up at who passed, except once a rig went by that was so outlandish colored it caught my eye like a bird will that's bright.

It was a little blue house on red wheels, and it had yellow curlicues all over it and some white words and a pale green door on the back end. It had boxes on top of it and pails and tools hanging under it, swinging and pretty often crashing together. It slowed down, like they all did—studying if to bother catching me, I figured —and I'd've turned my face away except I couldn't get my fill of that pretty rig. So it came about that when the driver turned his head to keep looking at me, I was gawking right at him. He gave me a fine smile, which I needed a lot right then, and it helped me so, I smiled back and when I rounded the next bend what should be pulled up on the roadside but that very same rig, and the driver lolling on the grass making music with a silver whistle.

He was younger than Pa, but older than me. About thirty, I guessed. I'd surely never seen the like of him before, but some things you just know, like he was a man Edward White wouldn't trust, and Pa would make fun of. A man that didn't belong in New England. Me, I never liked anybody so much, except Patience, and that was different. There was no doubt he was showing off for me, but since nobody'd ever bothered to show off for me before, I looked around to make sure there wasn't somebody else. There was nobody but me.

I felt the world go bright and the air get easy to breathe, and I just stood there hearing that silvery twiddly music, glad it was spring (it was May by then) and that I was me, and he was him.

"Runaway apprentice?" he asked.

"No."

"Run away from your father?"

"No."

"Had any dinner?"

"No."

He crossed his legs and went from sitting to standing in one easy-looking push. Pa or Edward White should try that. He wiped off his whistle and put it into a blue pouch the exact size of it. You could see from how he did it how much he cared about that whistle. I purely hated to see him put it away, except that then he opened the door of his rig—"van" he called it—and flopped down some steps down from inside. I stood so's to see in as much as I could without appearing too nosey.

He had the nicest, neatest, prettiest, best-rigged fine little snug home in there, with beds built like shelves one above another and covered with blue and white checkedy quilts tucked in at the edges, and little pretty curtains at the windows. I just wished I could tell my sisters about it, and Ma, and Patience. It made me lonesome to see that snug little home he had and have nobody to tell about it.

He brought out a basket with bread, cooked meat, and a pieplant pie he said he'd bought off a farmer's wife. My mouth started to water but he was a man that didn't pig into anything, so we waited till he'd spread a cloth and arranged everything on it and he'd prayed in a plain way, like to a person, "Lord, thank you for this food, such as it is. And thank you for this good boy to share it with."

It would've been so simple for him to make me stumble all over myself, being as I didn't know the first thing about manners and anybody could see he was a born gentleman and knew everything. But his little prayer, and the equal way he looked at me, like it mattered to have me like him, made me feel welcome and easy. I felt he didn't set himself up as my judge, or take pleasure in me making a mistake.

His horse was unhitched and chomping along in the grass. Not many men would unhitch for a short noon stop, just to make a beast more comfortable. I felt that this man cared about his horse, and about me, and that he didn't have any meanness in him. Pa'd always said you're better off in a bear trap than in the clutches of a Yankee peddler, and he must've based that on something, but it wasn't on this man.

"You peddle?" I asked. I'd been doing all the talking, about the troubles a boy can fall into on the road, so I figured I'd give him his turn.

He waited, just a touch, so I knew that those white words said his name and what he peddled and that I'd let him know I couldn't read. I was mortified, but he gave no sign of noticing beyond that little wait.

"Yes," he said. "I travel in books. I follow the circuit rider from court to court and lay out my wares on courthouse steps. Also tavern porches, on market days. My name's Daniel Peel. Dan Peel. They call me Parson Peel."

"A parson!"

Pa'd also always said that you're better off in a bear trap than in the clutches of a parson. Pa said parsons scare the dying and gouge the living, and that he'd have no traffic with them, not him nor his woman nor his children. Not even in Connecticut, where you just about had to. He said he didn't have to, no more than he had to bow down to a king, not in the United States, and there was General Washington to thank. Ma said Meeting's nice for singing and seeing folks, when you live off on a farm, and she'd kind of like it. You don't have to heed the words, she said. She'd like to have women in for quilting and all, but she couldn't without she went to Meeting and mingled and the women got to know her. Poor Ma, all shut up without a friend. Pa said we didn't need friends bad enough to go listen to a parson's lies and threats, which us children might take to heart and get scared sick over. I thought a lot on both sides of the question, without being able to make up my mind if Ma or Pa was right. No matter who was right, what Pa thought was what was done.

Even so, I'd seen parsons around—in the village, at the store, and once in a great while one would even come out to our place to pray over us and try to guide us.

Parson Peel said, "I was once a parson."

"Sawed from the wrong log for it," I said.

"So it worked out."

I'd meant to please him—who could want to be a born parson?—but he was sad. I liked the way his face showed gentleness, or laughiness, or sadness—whichever he felt.

He said, "I hoped it could be a happier thing than I'd ever seen it be."

Since we were both bound for Barrington, I rode with him. We sat up on his high seat and sped along so fine, with the pails and pans and jacks and chains rattling underneath, and us up there running our mouths. At Barrington I'd push on north and leave him to lay out his stock, so I felt I had to jam a whole life of talk into this little ride. I'm glad I didn't meet him on my first day out, or I might've thought everybody on the outside was like him. As it was, I knew enough to know I'd never see his like again.

I guess I must've talked about home, to make him say I'd missed the main things that civilize a man—school, church, society, books—so how did I come to be what I was? "You make me doubt my mission," he said. "Why aren't you a lout?"

"Maybe I am."

"No. I'd like to hear about your mother. Women civilize, too. What's she like?"

"Just a plain farmer woman. Tall. Got rough scratchy hands that scratch your chest when she rubs cough oil on you. I always liked that—like a cat's tongue."

"Does she pray?"

"Don't seem to."

"Does she sing?"

"She used to. Last few years she's been too sad."

"It's the sad that sing."

"Well, then she needs some new songs maybe. She likes to shut herself up alone. When the weather's right, she likes to go out to the woods. It makes Pa jumpy. He don't want her to. It's the only way she stands up to him. She goes anyhow. Once Rachel and me snuck after her, to see what she did. She just sat. We thought we heard her talking to herself, but we couldn't be sure."

"She was praying. She must have been," Parson said. He thought a while. Then he said, "People live their lives. Somehow they live their lives. It appears that songs and prayers will suffice. Does she tell her dreams? I have a dream book in my stock."

I didn't want to talk about Ma's dreams with Barrington so near, so I played I couldn't remember them.

"Do you get to York State? Did you ever see this Hudson River?" I asked.

"Yes, yes. I just came from there. Did she whip you?"

"*Whip* me? No!"

"You're surprised. As the Indians were. When the Indians saw us whipping our children, they thought at first that we must hate our children, but then they thought, no, no one can hate his child. They decided it must be a religious rite, to make the child hate this world and long for the next. We're a strange vicious people, Sam. I think about us. All the time. What do you think about? Swinging your ax, what do you think?"

"Of being—not alone—someday. Having my own land."

"You seem to think there's nothing a man can do but farm. A man can make shoes or build ships or peddle books or set bones or print newspapers or look at the stars—"

"For a *living?*"

"Look at the stars. For a living. Yes. Or make wheels or barrels or crocks or dishes—the world is very big and interesting. Make furniture or bricks or houses or trumpets or violins or pictures."

"I know somebody that makes pictures that make you laugh. Like in one, here's this woman just cut this man's head off, and he's laying there with just his neck, and she's walking away so ordinary with his head in a basket, like regular marketing."

The Parson laughed. I was kind of relieved, because the picture did begin to seem kind of not-laughable, at least the way I told it. "That's Judith and Holofernes," he said. "They're in the Bible. I don't seem to be able to stop teaching you. Indians, the Bible—I hope you don't mind."

"Oh, I like it. Judith and *who?* No, never mind. There's not time. Tell me about York State. Where would you leave this valley if you was me?"

"I'd have left it at Egremont, which is now behind us. It's where I came in."

"Oh," I groaned.

"The next good break in the hills, I'd say, is Stockbridge. A little easier to get lost from there is all."

"Stockbridge," I said, to fix it in my mind.

"Sam—" he said. His voice was different, about to ask me something. "—Sam, sometimes I have to carry a lot of money, and I must confess it makes me nervous, being alone then. And there's a lot of hefting book boxes around whenever I reach a town. I can usually hire some boy that's watching, you know, but—"

His voice faded out and we rode along with just the clanking. I thought about the things that happen to you when everybody thinks you're a runaway, and, I admit, how good it felt to be riding instead of walking, and how after a little while with Parson Peel I'd have a head full of thoughts to think. He might even teach me to read. It began to seem there was no real hurry about Genesee, especially since everybody I met stood in the way, and I'd missed Egremont.

"Where do you go winters?" I asked.

"To New-York City. To my wife and children and my study. Desk. Foolscap. Ink. Pen. I have some books by Parson Peel up in those boxes too."

I tried to picture myself in New-York City. I couldn't. I only knew it was a place I'd better see before I went so far I'd never get back.

"What say, Sam?"

"I want to learn to read," I said.

CHAPTER THREE

He set me to making letters on a slate, not in order like the alphabet but haphazard, like to spell out Sam and horse and road and tree, the things we saw. River, pan, meat, cloud, sky, hill. I pictured letters to put myself to sleep. Before long I could read most anything, and every day, with Parson hearing me, correcting or saying, "That's good," I got better and better at it. I was surprised how fast I learned. I'd always thought folks that could read must have some special gift, like for pretty singing or straight throwing. Parson said I was quick.

Nights we stopped by the road. Parson said he wouldn't sleep at an inn if paid to, and catch fleas and be snored on by ruffians three in a bed. The two of us, he said, could stand against anything that happened. He had a fine gun, all rubbed and fixed up with designs. I loaded and fired it a few times, to learn its quirks, and then I knew, too, we could face down any danger.

If there was no house handy to ask fire of, he could make it in a hurry. His trick was to rub gunpowder into his tinder, and the first strike of the flint would bring fire most every time. I suppose Pa knew that trick too, but couldn't spare the powder.

Then we'd cook supper, twice what we thought we'd want, to have the rest for next day's dinner. We didn't have just stews, but spitted meats as well, and he could make firebread as neat as Ma. One thing I draw the line at was unboiled salad. He claimed it's eaten unboiled in other lands, but he had such laughy eyes I knew he was just seeing how much he could push off on me. I sure didn't want us taking sick, and he as much as admitted he was relieved when I wouldn't go along with his nonsense.

While Parson cooked, I'd rub and curry the horse, which was a bay gelding named Potiphar, the first horse I ever had dealings with, being as Pa always kept cattle for draft. Parson wanted Potiphar treated very sweet and tender, to make it up to him for not having his own barn to hurry to and his own horse to be friends with. So I always took a good long time with Potiphar, rubbing and talking while he chomped his oats.

At first I worried Parson would find out I was a girl, living so close, sleeping so close, but he was a private man. He didn't show himself, or offer to look at me. I didn't see him without a shirt, and he took care of his bathing and other things by himself. I did the same. (I washed myself and my clothes a lot oftener than was healthy, for the sake of smelling as pleasant to sit next to as Parson did.) Many days, with me to drive, he went back to his bed and read or napped, which made it all right for me to go back some days too when I thought I'd better. As to shaving, it might've looked bad, me never needing to, but if Parson noticed he never mentioned. I sort of hoped he thought I shaved before he got up.

He did like his morning sleep, and from how late he stayed up he needed it. I'd fall off to sleep up on that top bed, tucked in all cozy, while he was still turning pages or writing. He wrote a letter to my folks, and great numbers to his wife, and even more to his printer saying the nation was perishing in darkness which only books could enlighten, or that he should have a higher percentage in commission, or why was his shipment not waiting for him at Adams? When he was writing he muttered it all as he went, so I kept track.

That cold summer may have been poor for ripening corn, but it was very good for burrowing deep into my bed and kissing my hands, which I named Patience, and dozing off to the little writing noises Parson made and the whale-oil smell of his lamp. I felt very near to happy, I think. I never knew how late he lasted.

"How did you do before you had me?" I asked.

"I had to keep farmer hours. I've needed this."

I won't say I understand why he liked lamplight better than the good light of the sun. He just did. I guess there was no harm in it except the expense, but he truly didn't belong in New England. By the time I felt free enough to give an opinion, I'd started thinking it was just one more lovable thing about him, and anyway handy for keeping it secret you're a girl.

Many a morning it was a good nine o'clock and I'd have us three hours along the road before I'd hear the van door slam and see Parson come running around to climb up beside me on the seat. I learned to have some coffee and bread there for him, and to keep my mouth shut till his eyes stopped watering and he felt like talking.

Usually the sign was he'd start to sing. There was one song he favored for morning that went

> *Whither goest thou, pilgrim stranger,*
> *Wandering through this lowly vale?*
> *Knowest thou not 'tis full of danger?*
> *And will not thy courage fail?*

That part in a little high mean worried voice, all weak and wavery and trying to make trouble while pretending to do good. Then the next part, Parson would stretch up and sing out all strong and happy and lots louder and faster:

No, I'm bound for the kingdom!
Will you go to glory with me?
Hallelujah! Praise the Lord!

Some days it made the hairs on my neck stand up. Not every day, of course. That would've been a good song to know when I was trudging alone up the Hooestennuc Valley.

He taught me lots of songs, or not exactly taught—sang them until I learned them, a little at a time. Lots were church songs, and some were just people songs, like "The Soldier Tired of War's Alarms" and "Sweet Nan of Hampton Green." One called "Water Parted from the Sea" made me so sad for Patience I almost didn't like to hear it, and yet something made me ask him to sing it oftener than any other song.

On the road that's how it was. It kind of hurt me that our time alone together on the road wasn't something he liked like I did. One time we were stopped in a little grove for the night and I felt sort of soppy because Parson was giving me a haircut and it reminded me of Ma and all, so I said, "I like it best like this, just the two of us." He kept quiet, just snipped. "I know you like town best. All them clever folks. Your own kind." (He kept on snipping.) "Do you *hear* me?"

"Yes. Everything."

Then he whisked and huffed the snippets off my neck, and gave me a little hit on the shoulder and went into the van and stayed there. When I went in to go to bed, quite a bit later, he was writing. Like always, he had his back to me and didn't look around. I knew he wasn't mad at me, but something made me want to play I thought so. After I was under the covers, I said, "Parson?"

"Uh?"

"You like me all right?"

"Of course I do. You know I do. Too much."

I laid there smiling to myself.

"Embarrassingly much," he said, and pretty soon I heard his pen start going again.

It makes me happy to remember the times on the road. I liked towns less, though they had some good things. I liked how the boys and dogs ran after our van, excited like over militia on Training Day, and looked up like they had an ambition to be me. I liked the stores that smelled of tea and spices and cloth and oil, and the few coins Parson gave me saying he'd come to feel he should, even though at first he'd felt the education he gave me was a fair exchange for my work. "I can't see you sniffing in a store without a coin to your name," he said, and somehow that didn't hurt my pride and I was glad to take the money. I liked seeing the fine houses and the tall churches, the streets that Potiphar made such a cloppety racket on, and that didn't get boggy even in the rain.

Since we couldn't well cook in courthouse squares, we ate at inns, and I liked that too, though Parson didn't. I'd never supposed there could be so many good things to eat, not all at one meal anyway. Like five or six kinds of meat, and all kinds of hot breads, and fruit, and honey and butter and cheese. All of it was made ready three times a day, even in midsummer, by gangs of blacks sweating away at a huge blazing fireplace in a kitchen I could no more hold my head in than if it was an oven, and couldn't take a breath in. I'd never seen blacks before, and even though I tried I couldn't get to know one. They worked too hard.

Parson said slavery was an abomination and would be the downfall of the United States, not only for the sin of it, but for how it kept boys like me from having the bottom to start at. The blacks could have the bottom if that was it. I knew I couldn't've faced that fire and done what they did.

They'd load the food in heaps on the big long tables, and then a bell would ring and the crowd—us too—would rush in, like starving, and hack and pull and stuff their mouths, till in fifteen minutes the platters would be bare and the floor covered with grease and bone. "Animals, we're animals," Parson would say, but I couldn't think of any animal that acted so bad. Maybe animals in strange lands do. Still I did like eating at inns, even though I wouldn't want it steady. I could hold my own and get my share. I'd bought myself a jackknife.

I got glum, a little, in towns. It wasn't the work that did it, though the work got heavy then, taking boxes of heavy books down from the top of the van and toting them to courthouse steps and all. I never would've noticed, I expect, except for that how likely a courthouse is to be built on a hill. It wasn't the work I minded, but the change that came over Parson Peel.

To be fair, I should take that back. He didn't change, except that he'd have on a ruffled shirt and a weskit with two rows of buttons and all to match. Inside himself he was just the same only to more people. He looked his kind interested look at lots of people, and listened as close to them as he ever did to me, leaning forward from the box he sat on, saying, "Tell me!" He taught and explained and smiled at everybody just like at me, and made them laugh like he did me, and it somehow, yes, I admit it, took me down. I didn't like it.

In town he'd get asked to people's houses too, and it never crossed his mind I might like to go along, or at least might like to be asked if only so I could say no. People who'd read the books he wrote would get to talking about one or another idea with him and then say, "Let's finish this up over a dram at home," and off Parson would go, saying, "Mind the shop, Sam," over his shoulder. Or he'd go off with a jag of dirty shirts and bedclothes to find someone to do them up for him, and it'd be hours before he came whistling back with a tale to tell, of what the washerwoman's life was like and if she prayed or sang or wept or had a friend or hoped for Heaven. He always

wanted to know the ways people kept going. No matter
how much the same the ways might be, he was always
interested. If it hadn't been I didn't want to be like Pa or
Edward White, I might've thought Parson should take
some of that interest in his business.

Sometimes I felt tempted to mess up the business, but
I never did because I was proud, too, that I could read
enough to give people the book they asked for, and change
money, and that Parson trusted me. Business was good.
I wouldn't't've believed, especially in a hard summer, that
people would turn over their hard-earned money for what
couldn't feed or clothe or shelter them, for just words
such as they could set down themselves if their arm
could stand the strain. Ma always said, "Talk's free," and
what's writing but just another form of talk? As well try
to sell air, I would've thought, except I could see for
myself the hunger people felt for our wares—not just
*Bard's Compendium of the Theory and Practice of Mid-
wifery,* or guides to the wilderness, which made some
sense, but history and biography and made-up stories and
rhymes, Bibles and dictionaries and *thoughts.* All these
were bought by plain sensible people, as well as fine
folk.

I've been putting-off telling it, but there was a problem
about fights too. I mean, in town I'd get in fights. Back
where I said how boys ran after us? It wasn't only that,
which I liked. They hung around the van too, as I guess
they couldn't help, and sometimes I let myself be drawn
into a little bragging about Parson, and one thing would
lead to another, and anyway it's touchy business being
envied, so oftener than I care to recollect, there'd be the
boys drawing back to make room for a fair fight, just a
solid circle with me and somebody else blocked up in it
and everybody yelling, "Hit 'im! Git 'im!" It was just
sport for them, no real hard feelings, just exercise, but
it was hard on me. I learned not to keep getting up as
soon as I could for as long as I could, so I didn't get

hurt much. And little as I thought he could, Parson taught me a few ways to make a throw so I didn't even necessarily lose. But I didn't like fighting. It wasn't just how me being female might come out. I didn't *like* to fight. I never really knew for sure till then how much I had the feelings of a woman, and not only that but I rated a woman's feelings higher.

We were zigzagging across Massachusetts, no rush, just tending generally east with the idea of finally hitting the Boston Post Road back to New-York City in the fall. I was always ready to push on before Parson was, and get him to myself again. He seemed glad enough to linger three or four days, to sell a little more, or talk, or wait for the stage to bring him letters and more stock.

After a town he'd have things to think over and write down. I'd keep quiet and stay out of his way until he was ready to look at me and talk again.

When he would talk, it was wonderful. His mind was so full but still easy, and I doubt there was anything he didn't know something about. The littlest thing reminded him, like Potiphar would shrug off a fly and Parson would tell me about the Hindoos who wouldn't kill a fly, and from that to India, to how Columbus was looking for India when he found us, to how Columbus went home from his second voyage a prisoner in chains, to how up until Christianity everybody knew the earth was round, to how the planets swim around the sun, to how some people think the places the planets are when you're born make a mark on you that you never get over. Like I was born when the sun was in a place called Leo and I have more in common with other people of Leo than with my own family. All from a fly on Potiphar's hide. Patience was born when the sun was at Aquarius. Parson's sun was in Gemini.

I loved his talk, but one day when I clapped him on the back and said so, plain out, "I love your talk," he climbed down and stayed in the van all day. I hardly got a glimpse of him all that day, though he claimed he wasn't sick.

Next day it was midmorning before he got up beside me and yet he still acted sleepy. He never did sing or play his flute, all that day. I read my lesson to him, but I doubt he listened. He was in some kind of deep sad thought, so I pushed my leg over closer, like a dog will put its head in your lap when it sees you need comfort.

"Sam, I wish I believed you were twenty-two."

"I am. I was twenty-two on the thirty-first of July."

"Will you swear it?"

I was sure puzzled but I said, "Yes, I swear it."

"I'd like to stop sitting on my hands. I'm very tired of sitting on my hands."

"I thought that was just your way."

"Just lately."

Had he guessed I was a woman? I took my leg back from pushing his, and slid over to my edge of the seat.

"Have you changed your mind?" he asked.

"What about?"

"About what we have."

"No."

He put his hand on my knee.

"Parson!"

"Are you going to pretend that you don't care for me?"

"Not like that. Not that way. I can't."

"Can't or not, you do, and I do."

"Oh, no, Parson."

I leaned so far away from him I started to fall off the seat. He caught me and then kept his arm across my shoulder even after I had my balance back.

"I suppose you think men don't do this," he said. "I assure you that men have loved and embraced each other since the beginning of time."

I knew how he liked to tell whoppers about other lands, but he didn't have a laughy way this time. I didn't know what to believe or think or do. I kept remembering Pa's last warning to me, but would it apply in a case like this? I decided to say no more and hope for the best.

Parson took his arm away and kept to his own side of the seat. I chanced a little look at him. "Ah, Sam," he said, "be nothing but a good boy. Scatter bastards all the way to Genesee, like a real American."

He'd never talked like that before, that backwards mean way. He even took a crack at Potiphar with the whip I'd always taken to be just an ornament. Potiphar was so surprised he looked around.

"Parson, don't be riled," I said. "I can't help it."

"Yes you can. You could help it very easily. You could consider that I might be telling you the truth. This is a common natural thing. Men love each other, Sam."

"Stop calling me Sam. I'm Sarah."

CHAPTER FOUR

I swear Parson was surprised, even if he did claim not. He stared so before he started laughing, about how you laugh when you drop something on your foot.

"Did you really take me in, for one single minute?" he said. "Didn't I know? Somehow? Of course I must have. It's so easy to see."

I said, "Maybe it's why you—had feeling?"

"No, no," he said, like brushing off a skeeter. I was used to having him give a little thought to what I said. And even if I didn't want him pestering me, it took me down some to think it would be plumb simple for him not to.

I said, "Maybe you won't want me around now."

"My dear—girl! Do you think I feel no responsibility towards you after taking you a hundred miles out of your way?"

"Well, don't worry about that. I don't regret. It's just that we might not be easy together, now."

"I feel completely comfortable. More so than before," Parson said. It seemed to be true, and I mostly wanted it to be. How could he care for me as a woman when he already had a wife? So we stayed on our way together.

But differences came creeping in, like Parson started helping with the book boxes, and he never said another

cuss word in my hearing, and I think a little at a time
he stopped educating me. I mean, he seemed to stop saying
whatever came into his head. There'd be little waits, it
seemed to me, while he thought out what it was fitting
or useful for a woman to know. He didn't leave me alone
nights if there looked to be a fight coming up.

I thought, well, good and bad've come of this. I liked
the extra care and company he gave me, but then I began
to see that he wasn't getting the good of his summer if he
didn't feel free to have a dram and talk wherever he went,
whenever he felt like it. I found that it's worse than lonesome to be with somebody that would rather be someplace
else, even when he keeps still about it and acts kind. I
found that all the changes were bad. Not one was good.

I'm not faulting Parson nor blaming myself either.
I'm just trying to tell how it went. You wouldn't think just
a word could change a whole friendship like that. I didn't
get weak and gal-ish. Nothing happened but a word. But
we couldn't fix it, and I knew I had to leave Parson. I
knew he would never ask me to, and that I could take
advantage of his kind heart for a long time, but I had my
pride and my own life to make.

Summer being over, and Genesee further away than
before, I decided I had to stay with him to New-York and
work the winter there and hope to get started off early
the next spring. I remember steering Potiphar along the
Boston Post Road, along the Connecticut shore heading
west for New-York, and making the plan while Parson
slept. There'd be lots a boy could do in a city like that.
Deliver wood, tend horses, carry messages. I didn't worry
I might have to turn to Parson and bother him in his home.
I knew I wouldn't.

I wonder if it was how Potiphar perked up because he
knew he was going home, that put it on my mind how
my home was off that way too. Every day took us closer,
and I got nervous, afraid what I might do, because I was

so excited. I said a little of it to Parson, because it was so much on my mind, and he told me a story about a sea captain that had his sailors stuff their ears with wax and tie him to the mast so he could listen to the marimaids singing without doing what they told him to. They wanted him to run his ship on the rocks.

I said that was it all right, that was just how I felt, just like that captain. "I sure wish you'd tie me to the whipple tree or lock the van door on me or something," I said. Because I wouldn't be able to leave home again as ignorant and hopeful as I was the first time, and there was the whole misery of Patience and how she didn't mean what I did or feel what I did or else she could never've said what she did at the end.

I didn't tell Parson much about Patience. I just said there was somebody there. I lost her for telling Rachel, and I was scared to tell again, even somebody that didn't know her.

Either Parson didn't take me serious, or he halfway wanted me to go. Or maybe he thought I'd calm down once we crossed the Hooestennuc and it looked like I'd stay. I thought my throat would break when we crossed that river, but we bedded down for the night the same as always and next morning pushed on.

And just west of Stratford I left Potiphar in charge of himself, because I knew a stop would wake up Parson, and I got my clothes and gear out of the van, and wrote on my slate, "Gone home," and looked at Parson asleep and felt sad. I went around and stopped Potiphar and weighted his lines with a rock, and gave his fine big round rump a pat.

Parson, as I kind of knew he would be, was looking out the window by then. He rapped so I went around back to the door. He opened it. "I'm going home," I said.

"So I see. But without goodbye?"

"I just can't hardly stand goodbyes."

"How far will you be by dark?"

"All the way, if I step along."

"I wonder if I should take you."

"Potiphar wouldn't stand for that, smelling home like he does. I'll be just fine."

"I'll give you some food at least," he said.

I waited in the doorway with my back to him, listening to him dig around.

When he came back he roughed my hair and said, "Here's some dinner. And here's the number of my house. And here's something to remember me by." It was the book he'd been hearing me read from, *Garvey's Speller and Reader*. It gave me tears in my eyes, but just eyes— not enough to run down.

"I'll never see your like again," I said.

He said, "You know, I won't see your like, either." I think he just then knew that.

I stuffed his gifts inside my shirt and started back along the road. I needed the river to guide myself home.

Inland from the Sound there'd been hard frosts. The leaves had all turned bright, so pretty they made me sad. The air smelled cidery from windfall apples. I didn't know where to turn my thoughts to get away from sadness and worry and guilt. Remembering Parson had its drawbacks just then, with parting so new. Thinking ahead to what Pa'd say about me coming back after the corn was cut and shocked, the year's field work all but done, was bad too. Worst was the thought of Patience, but she's what I mostly thought of, and the kiss she might give me, or might not. One of my feet knew she'd kiss me, and the other was sick because it knew she wouldn't. I had no opinion of my own. All I knew was how dry my mouth was.

CHAPTER FIVE

I ached to go right straight to Patience, not go home first at all, but I was dirty from the day on the road, and my mouth tasted gluey from worrying and hoping all day, not fit to kiss. I didn't dare make any more mistakes about Patience. She cared what people thought, and what would people think of a boy-girl that showed up scared and dusty at twilight like the soldier tired of war's alarms? So I took myself in hand and went home.

The dogs heard me and trotted out meaning business, but then they knew me and started yelping and jumping on me and slobbering all over me and running in circles. Near knocked me down, but they made me feel better. Then out came my folks, not so spry as the dogs but in the same spirit. They hugged me, all that could, and hugged each other when there wasn't hugging room left on me and called my name and laughed and cried. I was welcome. I had a place, just like Pa'd said.

We went inside. They'd been at supper. Rachel filled a plate for me. I played I didn't see her take from others to do it. They wanted to give me something, so I couldn't make a fuss. The food seemed odd, without the extra leaves and things Parson always put in, just boiled and salted.

I couldn't get over how small and dark and poor the

house was, and how maybe it was up to me to make it better. Maybe I'd have to stay my whole life here, doing my part for them.

Their voices sounded odd. They said mine did. They wanted to hear everything. Who was this Daniel Peel that wrote to them? I talked and talked, because they expected me to. They knew me to be a talker, and I think I still was, but not with them. I mean, not natural like before. Because now I had secrets from them. Like, Pa said, "Did you let on you're a gal?" and I said—"No."

"I'm not plain thankful to that man," Pa said. "Without him you'd've been back sooner. I'd've never let you go except I figured you'd be right back. Now you think it's easy on the road. You didn't learn a thing."

"I learned to read, Pa. And I can teach you all. Parson gave me a book."

"Learn to read and you want books," Pa said. "One more fool thing to want and not get. I won't have it." His face was so mulish I quit for then. I was too tired to explain to him that he was perishing in darkness.

I went up to bed. Rachel came too. It was her first chance at me alone. She bundled up against me. I let her. I liked it. I found I didn't hold it against her anymore, what she'd done. But all the same I wasn't about to make the same mistake twice.

I didn't ask for news of Patience, but Rachel gave it anyhow, what she had. "Patience White kept school summer term," she said. I hid that I was interested, but Rachel's head was on my heart, which thumped. "When that letter come, from Daniel Peel, I took and showed it to her."

"Is she who read it to you?"

"No. Pa got somebody in town. Afterwards I took it."

I didn't ask how Patience was, was she glad for news of me, was she healthy, was she happy? (Oh, let her not be happy till it's me that makes her be!)

Rachel said, "Did you find someone else to care for, on the road?"

"Parson. I care for Parson," I said.

"But he's married," Rachel said.

"I can't help that," I said, chokey.

I don't know why people think I can't be sly. They think I'm simple like a white plate, but how was that for sly?

That chokiness made Rachel fancy a whole tale, of me caring more and more for Parson but trapped in my lie of being a boy, kept from speaking, suffering so much I finally had to leave him. I just laid there holding her and letting her tell it, and letting my thoughts go to Patience so Rachel would think the thump in my heart was for Parson.

"See, all you needed was the right kind of a man," Rachel said. "You was always a woman at heart."

"Too much," I said. Oh, sly.

"That with Patience White was just her being the first outside one to show you kindness."

"There was Simon," I said, to sound honest to a fault. Simon was a young man that stopped for food at our place on his way up the valley, and took a liking to me and wanted me to marry him and go along. I thought some of doing it, because I liked him, but as soon as he kissed me I knew I couldn't live a life where that happened all the time.

"Simon wasn't much," Rachel said.

"No."

Rachel said, "Patience White——" I thought of Simon to slow my heart down "——she said to let her know anything we heard from you. She said she was sorry the two of you'd had differences. Did you?"

"Oh, not to speak of. I expect I better get over to see her one of these days," I said, offhand, thinking of Simon.

With everybody so glad to see me, I maybe could've loafed a few days, but I rolled myself out next morning

with the rest of them, and started three days of hauling
in corn. I wanted to do my part so I could feel free Sunday afternoon to go to Patience. There was no use going
sooner, knowing she'd be too bound up in family work to
see me. Fall's when woman's work is heaviest, with all
the winter food to lay by.

I thought and thought how Sunday I'd borrow a dress
off Ma and cover my cropped head in a bonnet and speak
ladylike. All told, do nothing to make Patience ashamed
of me. I thought up good topics to speak on, such as
what the ladies in Massachusetts wore—women talk. I
thought how if Pa said something against going, I'd just
look surprised and say, "Why, I got nothing against her,"
and if he went on from there I'd say, "Oh, that! That
was nothing." And if he beat me again to keep me from
her, I'd try one of the throws Parson taught me.

By Saturday afternoon I'd got myself into a fine state
with all this figuring. I was in the field with my sister
Mary. She was driving the cart and I was heaving corn up
onto it. She was coming along all right as a boy, but we
still gave her the easiest jobs.

I had sweat in my eyes, but Mary could see fine and
was higher up, so she was the first to notice Patience
coming across the field to us. Mary said, "Who's that with
the girls?" Even while I wiped my eyes, I somehow knew,
and then I saw the sun on that bright fox hair, and that
good little busy step, and my sisters all pushing to be the
ones to hold her hands.

I lit off towards her as fast as I could run, which was
pretty fast, but then as I got nearer I remembered how
I had bare feet and a sweaty shirt so my running dwindled
off and I stopped and stood there looking at her.

"Yo, Sarah!" she called. I would've answered but I
couldn't.

"We've got Miss White, Miss White!" my sisters kept
yelling. All I wanted to do was fall on my knees.

Then she was so close I could see her freckles. "I just

heard that you're back," she said. The girls still had both
her hands so there was none for me.

I swallowed and nodded. It was like being with Parson
hadn't taught me a thing about not being a bumpkin.

She said, "I'm glad you're home. Will you come by my
place tomorrow?"

I nodded.

"Can we come?" my sisters said. "Can we come?"

"No, babies. Not this time," Patience said.

They felt the iron schoolmarm under all her sweetness
and said no more.

Patience said, "I can't stay. I left a hundred things un-
done. I just had to say I'm glad you're back. Come after
noon. I'll be at Meeting in the morning. If I'm not home
yet when you get there, go on inside."

I walked to the road with her, pushed entirely away
from her by my sisters of course, and yet I felt peacefuller
than I would've expected to. I didn't need to touch her if
I knew I was welcome.

Sunday noon, decked out according to my plan, I
started for Patience's place. Nobody tried to stop me or
go along. Maybe Rachel'd explained that I was suffering
over Parson, or maybe Pa'd decided that what's not
flattered by notice will go away. I don't know. I never
asked and they never said.

I tried to walk slow, because Patience wouldn't be home
yet anyhow, but naturally I just tore along. I got there.
Her house seemed different, smallish and plain, not
scarey. That hired man, Tobe, called off the dogs and
said, "Go on along in. She said to look for you." Parson
would've said, "Thank you," so I did too.

I went on inside to wait for Patience. It got me by the
throat to see the bench and the table and like that. I
came very near to kissing the bench, but I didn't want
to let myself out of hand in case Patience just wanted
to be ordinary friends. I would be anything to Patience she

wanted me to be, and do anything she wanted, even stay away if, God forbid, she wanted that. And I wouldn't kiss her bench or sniff at her clothes or hug her pillow until she gave some sign to let me.

I sat at the table where I could look out the window. I kept the bonnet on so she'd see I'd made a good appearance for Tobe. It would've looked good to be found reading, but I also wanted to show that I could be trusted in a house not to go looking for books where I hadn't been asked to. It's likely I couldn't've kept my eyes on words anyhow, with the yard to watch for her coming.

After almost longer than I could stand, which maybe wasn't really long at all, she was there, jumping down before the horses stopped, and I breathed careful and looked at the door but didn't stand up.

She came in. "You're here," she said.

"Yes."

She hung her bonnet and cloak on the pegs. So slow. And asked for my bonnet and cloak and took them without looking at me or touching me and hung them slow too. She asked did I want tea? cider?

"No, nothing," I said, to lose no more time.

But she said, "Cider for me, I think," and she took a pitcher to the cellar and took so long to come back I could've groaned. What made her jump down before the horses stopped? Thirsty?

At last she sat across the table from me, with her hands on the pitcher. I felt her looking at me. I raised my eyes to find out my fate. She had no smile for me. I was afraid.

I looked on up to her eyes and held there steady, thinking pretty soon she'd look away, and then when I knew she wouldn't the silver thread our eyes were joined by began to hum like far-off bees. I felt my soul melt and flow out along it. I felt my heart melt and drip off my fingertips.

I am trying to tell exactly true.

"Do you forgive me?" she whispered.

"Yes." I wanted to say more. I couldn't, but it was enough.

We stayed that way a time that can't be said the ordinary way. One minute—twenty minutes—a thousand years—I don't know.

I felt her take my hand. I heard her say, "Come on," and I stood up ready to go anywhere, to her bed or off a cliff or into the fire, anywhere she took me. My eyes were blurry and blind. Maybe she was sending me home. I stumbled along where she led me, and stopped because I bumped something. It was Patience herself, turned to me, arms open to hold me, face up to be kissed, but I couldn't kiss her until my feeling got less. I stood there just holding her, until time got ordinary and earthly things got possible, like kisses and smiles and words.

I held her chin in my hand and moved her face to make her mouth be where I wanted it, and bent my head down. She is exactly the right height to bend to, and the right plumpness to fill my arm. I could've stood kissing her there for the rest of my life, but my knees went weak and I had to look around for a place to go. The closest place was the floor, but I couldn't put her where she might not be comfortable. I just wouldn't lose being pressed front to front by taking her to the bench.

It was getting to be a severe puzzle, with my knees giving out. I wasn't bold enough to take her to her bed, but then she, who for all her womanly ways was always bolder than me, took me to bed. Into the bedroom and up onto that high white feathery bed. She stretched out and patted beside her to show me my place, and I went into it. I propped myself up on my elbow and looked down at her and words like hallelujah and glory kept coming to me. What do folks that never went around with an unfrocked parson think at a time like that?

I put my cheek against hers. It felt as good as a kiss. Oh what else is as soft and firm and downy smooth and cool as a woman's cheek? It made me proud that mine was the same and I could give it to her.

"Stop that silly smiling," she said. She felt it in my cheek.

"I can't. I can't. I'm happy."

And she was smiling too, so who was she to talk?

I said, "When you came across the field yesterday, I couldn't believe I ever kissed you, or ever would."

"But I believed it," she said.

"What made you—" I began, and then I couldn't ask it after all. She knew anyway.

She said, "I asked myself what was the worst thing that could happen to me. So then it was all clear and easy. Losing you, that was the worst. I can't remember why I drove you away. Was it just to keep what I never liked anyway? I don't know why I didn't go with you."

"Scared, that's all," I said. "If I'd had sense enough I would've been too."

She said, "Don't talk that way," and turned her face to kiss.

I kissed her, but I also managed, between kisses, to explain that boys and penniless women don't fare so easy on the way west, and they should thank the stars they got born under for a room and a tall soft bed to kiss on. "There's nothing out west to beat this," I said.

How was it possible to stand up and walk to the pegs and put my wraps on? I said, to head her off from warning me, which I couldn't've stood, "This time I won't tell."

"As you wish," she said. I didn't believe her. Even if I wished to tell, I'd better not. I knew my lamb that much. But I liked having her say it like I had a choice: "As you wish."

I couldn't think of anything to want beyond what that day marked the start of. There was good hard work all week, and then those wonderful Sunday afternoons when I could hold Patience and lean over her face trying to find the exact name for the brown of her eyes, and studying her ear with the tip of my tongue, and feeling her clean breath on me, learning how born to fit her eyelid my mouth was, watching the daylight fade across her face. I learned the use of being beautiful. I got beautiful myself, or so she said. I was perfectly happy. A person would have to be bolder than me to imagine something beyond perfect happiness and wish for it.

But I already said, Patience is bolder.

At first I didn't know it was more she wanted. I thought maybe it was less, or different. Before long it was clear something was amiss. She got so she didn't pay attention like I did. I always kept one eye open a crack, to look, because being looked at that way is the use of being beautiful, and on our fifth Sunday during one of our kisses, she wasn't looking back at me, and I swear she was *thinking*. I'd suspected her of it before, but this time there was no mistaking it.

I backed right off, for I knew from Simon how a kiss feels when you don't want it and I'd rather die than have somebody feel that way from any doing of mine. I got across the bed from her, flat on my back, and looked at the ceiling.

"We don't need to," I said. "Don't think just cause you started you've got to keep on."

"Do you think you could stop now?"

"If you wanted." It was true that if she wanted to stop I'd have to slit my throat, but I didn't see that as needing to be said. If she could stop, I could work out a way of stopping too without bothering her about it.

"You think so?" she said, in a wonderful scarey dangerous way, like she was going to prove to me I couldn't stop.

"I'd have to, if you wanted to," I said.

She said, "I don't want to stop." She rolled up close to me. "I want to start." Her face was above me then, the tables turned, and I wondered did it feel that way to her when I leaned over her, and if it did how could her thoughts wander? She kissed me, a sweet soft cozy kiss, and drew back and said, "Recognize it?"

I shook my head.

"You should. It's Our Kiss."

"It's good."

"Yes. And so's this." I thought, no, no, gentle is better, I can't feel that your lips are soft, I can't remember that you are Patience and that I love you, and then I realized I'd shut my eyes. So I opened them. I saw her freckles and her eyebrows and her frown. Her thoughts didn't wander. I reached up to touch her hair, which I loved the red of, the snappiness of, softness of, but she caught my wrist and held it. She said, "Do nothing." I knew she was cross at breaking the kiss to say that, and I thought, I have to find a way to show you that I am yours and have no wishes apart from yours, and the thought caused my body to find a way, which later on we made a name for. We called it melting.

Then she was gentle and made lots of soft ways to kiss and touch me. Her face was so proud. I just stayed still, smiling a little inner smile I hid from her and feeling that she was mine too, and that she couldn't stop now either.

When we got back to where we could smile real smiles, she said, "Now stop thinking we can stop and start thinking what we're going to do about it."

"What's there to do, but keep on doing it?"

She didn't move, but I felt her go away from me. "Just like this?" she asked in a tone of voice that made me scared to admit, yes, that was what I had in mind—just like this, just like this. I was scared. What was the matter with just like this? Why didn't it make her happy? Was there something she liked better she was comparing it to? Then I thought maybe she wanted to have the feeling in her body that I'd had, so I tried to give it to her, but she said, "It's getting late. You have to go," and even though I said, "I don't care—I don't care," she turned away from me, saying, "Go."

I put my wraps on but I couldn't let the best time of all end so miserable, so I went again to the bed where she was still curled up with her back to me and I said, "Next Sunday?"

"Yes, of course," she said, but in a way that kept me just as scared.

"Patience, Patience, what do you want?"

"Go home. It's getting dark," she said, and I didn't know what else to do so I went.

My heart was in my throat all week, and what made it worst was needing to play nothing was wrong, which is hard when you can't eat and can't sleep and it's chancey can you keep your temper. I finally just took the ax and went out to work on the new field, to have a time alone. There was some comfort in laying all my strength behind the ax. It was just comfort enough to keep me from tipping up my chin and howling.

I studied and studied on what was wrong, until I figured out what the trouble was, Patience thought it was wicked, what we did. She could kiss me, because women always kissed, and she didn't have to admit how different our kisses felt, but when the feeling got out of our hearts and went everywhere, all over us, then it was different and no getting out of admitting it.

I remembered Parson saying how the whole idea behind making this country was to stamp out wickedness, and how you know what's wicked is whatever feels good. I could see how Patience could have wickedness come to her mind, just home from Meeting and all. I didn't fault her. I set myself to bear giving up and giving up until we got back to something she could do without feeling wicked.

Next Sunday when I got there, Patience wasn't home

yet. She pretty often wasn't. Like always when she wasn't, I took my shoes off and got into her bed to wait. I liked having a place warmed up for her when she came in cold. It was winter by then. I thought how I would wrap myself around her and hold her hands and warm them with my mouth.

At last she came. She bent and kissed me. I started to go wild inside. It was so different when I looked up at her instead of down. I held her to try to make it last, but she stopped and I had to let her go. Instead of getting in with me she sat in a chair beside the bed. She didn't look happy.

"We have to talk," she said.

"All right," I said. I was afraid.

"There's been too much bed and not enough talk."

I said, "We could talk in bed."

She smiled a little, saying, "I know you better than that."

The way she said it wasn't exactly mean. It wasn't exactly like she didn't love me. It was like she was older than me, like not plain equal. It got my pride up. If it was just me we went to bed for, we didn't have to go. I jumped out like the bed was afire and grabbed my shoes and went out to the kitchen.

Right away I stopped being riled and wished I could figure out a way to get back, and then I remembered maybe bed was what worried Patience and made her feel wicked and maybe it was all to the good that I'd jumped out before I knew what I was doing, because I couldn't've done it otherwise and maybe it had to be done. Bed could be given up. Bed was a lot to ask.

Patience came in and sat down behind her spinning wheel. It was like a fence between us. She whirled it a little, for something to do, but she didn't spin because it was Sunday.

"I find that I can still think," she said.

I waited.

She said, "Even after what happened last time, I can think. And I think—I—don't—like it—this way."

I dropped my shoes and covered my face with my hands. That wasn't enough so I ran into her parlor and stood facing into the corner. I blocked up my mouth with my arm.

I heard her come and stand behind me. "Don't," she said. "Don't hurt me like this."

I started making a noise that didn't stop. From sort of faraway I listened to it. It sounded quite a lot like laughing. I didn't turn around. I heard Patience go away.

When I could I went back to my shoes. I felt burny and dried out, but at the sight of Patience a whole new batch of tears came pouring down. I kept quiet, though. I sat down to put my shoes on. She came and stood in front of me so close I couldn't bend down.

She said, "Is this what you want? Falling on each other like starving animals once a week?"

"We don't. We never did," I found I could say.

"We will."

So all my tears and hurt stopped like a line storm, like coming to a wall.

"Will we?"

"You know it. And you're actually glad." She smiled, lopsided. She called me wench and kissed me and I relaxed my neck and let my head fall back and held on, getting ready for the wonderful thing to happen.

Then I thought maybe it was what she meant by animals, and I thought I'd better show her it didn't have to happen every time she kissed me. Otherwise she might quit kissing me, besides not getting into bed with me.

The very exact second I decided I wouldn't let my body do that, she straightened up. I waited like a baby bird. She didn't bend down again, so I started feeling foolish. I shut my mouth and tried to look sensible.

Being sensible, I said, "Reckon we never did talk like you said you wanted."

"I was going to be like a father and ask your intentions, but I begin to think you haven't any."

"You mean, like plans?"

"Like plans."

"No, I guess not. Except just keep on loving you."

"Every week," she said so soft and flat I couldn't tell if she meant it good or bad.

"If that's too much, it wouldn't need to be that much. I could get along on less." I explained it all very fast, not to leave her in doubt an extra minute. "I know once a week's a lot to ask."

She just shook her head like at a puzzle she gave up on.

BOOK THREE

Patience

CHAPTER ONE

You are forlorn on my bench, seeking yet more ways to reassure me that you don't want me very much or need me very often. When I grumble at our half-loaf, you offer me a crumb. When I ask to launch our ship, you suggest we fish the millpond with it. You do without, in everything, until you forget how to want. Luckily, I can be willful for two.

I say, "Have you forgotten Genesee?"

"Not exactly."

"Have you given it up?"

"You might say." (Your mouth so dry I can hear your tongue pulling away from the roof of it.)

"Why?"

"I learned something, out there trying."

"I learned something, staying here. I want to go. I want our home."

I think I imagined you'd be overjoyed at that. I think I thought it was your not knowing exactly what I wanted that tied your tongue. But your face is far from happy. Given years enough, and your help, I may grow humble.

I say, "Don't *you?*" When you don't answer, I kneel and put my arms around you, saying, "Don't you? Darling, don't you?"

You say, "It's like lots of things I might want. No use thinking on it."

Who is this cautious unhoping young woman? Where is the hero who bore such batterings for love and stood up before witnesses to ask me to be a hero too? And I am a hero now. Can't you see? We can be an army of two. We can be Plato's perfect army: lovers, who will never behave dishonorably in each other's sight, and invincible. Let the world either kill us or grow accustomed to us; here we stand.

I say, "I think there's a use in thinking about our home."

"When we can't have it?"

"The first step is to think about it. Shall I tell you what it looks like? Or what happens inside it?"

You like the game. You choose what happens.

"In the first place, I am never on my knees."

"Get up, oh get up," you say.

I take you to my bed. Your head with its half-grown child-like hair is on my pillow. I make us a tent with the covers. I am the pole. Slanting. A very low tent, an almost horizontal pole. Ah, I was right before. Bed is a place we do not talk. I bend down the cloth that divides us and find (again) the tanned V the sun made at the base of your throat last summer. I kiss the V and then the pure creamy skin beside it, that the sun never saw. (And I begin to wonder, who has seen it? There must be no one but me.)

"This happens in our house," I say. "Every day. Without the cloth, of course. Unless we decide we prefer cloth. I may find that I love your skin best when I must search for it."

In dreaming as in everything you are a quick pupil. You are dreaming already, but I was never so awake. I miss nothing. I gaze down at you, watching as you turn your head to hide your face from me, feeling the wave in you. Someday, when you are a hero again, I will give the same to you.

But afterwards you still say—I have not succeeded in making you reckless—"We really can't, you know."

"Yes we can."

"No. It's too hard. I'm not a man."

"No indeed," I say, smiling, I hope, wickedly.

"I'm not even very much like a man."

"Not at all. No, not at all."

"I haven't got everybody backing me up like a man, and I'm not strong enough by myself."

"You're not by yourself."

"I won't take you to wild country and I won't let you think I'm going to. We're better off right here."

Travel has not been good for you. Once you thought I knew more of the world than you did.

You say, "You think we can go off without a cent and everybody against us and you're wrong."

"My brother will help us."

"Not likely."

"Yes. He was moved. You impressed him. Tell me you want our home, and I'll ask him to help us."

"Maybe he will, and maybe he'll set the dogs on me, and maybe he'll tell Pa, and maybe you'll find you care what people think."

So that's it! Yes, of course. But it takes more than one whimper to make a coward. I added a cubit to my stature by taking thought.

"Try me!" I say. (Yes, I need to be tried. How can I know, myself, until I am tried?)

"Let's just stay like this," you say. "Can't we? I've been so happy. This is so much more than I ever thought a person could have. Why do we have to fight with each other, and ask for more? Who do you know that's got more?"

Nobody. But I know someone who will have more, and it is I.

"Come tomorrow," I say.

"Tomorrow! You're busy all day, same as me."

"In the evening."

"It'd look—it'd call attention."

"Don't worry. Bring somebody. A sister."

"I'd have to explain about us."

"No you wouldn't."

"Then nothing could happen."

"It doesn't matter. I have to see you more. Every day."

"You want me out on the road at night in the cold?"

"Yes!"

You bow your head. Are you hurt? Are you offended? I don't care. You submit. I am not wrong about what that wave meant. You will be here tomorrow.

I say, "Tell them you need help with reading. Or else the truth. Either."

You leave me. I feel the cold air like a sword where your warmth has been. You tear my whole front open when you cease to lie along it. My skin goes with you. I could bleed to death.

You are here. I make the proper exclamations and kiss, indifferently, the air beside your cheek. I turn to greet whichever sister you brought, who hangs back shyly in the dark hallway. "Come in, come in," I say, and she does. It is your mother.

How can I bear her unease? I must end it. I set myself to warm and welcome her, cherish her. My mother-in-law unaware. When she is seated, trying to be no trouble, take up no space, I say, "We must have a fire in the parlor," and though she says she's fine, she's cozy, goodness, I say, "It'll only take a few minutes."

I spread my fingers in your hair, saying, "Come help me. The kitchen's good enough for *you,* but not your mother." Again she says there's no need, goodness, but I think she is flattered. I hope I detect it.

You with wood, I with coals, we go to the parlor, and

to keep the cold breath of it from your mother we have to shut the door of course. I see your face in the glow of the coals. You make the fire .

I like you in these clothes, your work clothes, breeches and shirt. You are graceful in them. My lovely tall cat.

"Is it all right I brought her?" you murmur.

"Of course. What did you tell her?"

"I said you think I need more reading lessons."

"And indeed I do think so, probably."

I tilt my chin up for your kiss, but your lips are stiff and nervous. I slap, not hard, your bottom, saying, "Pay attention to what you're doing. I won't let you go till you make my toes tingle." You try again. It's no use. You are thinking of your mother.

"At least I have my memories," I say, and though you try to keep me and explain, I go back to your mother.

I make tea for her and talk with her. We speak of seasonable and unseasonable. Then, to frighten you, I say, "Mrs. Dowling, I wonder if I dare share with you a vice I learned at school? We can read another time. This evening I want to share with you."

I think she is almost disappointed when the vice is only cards. She's not as stern against vice as you seem to think.

I teach the two of you to play Hearts. You learn fast, she less so, but since she loves you she takes no offense.

"Was Sarah always so easy to teach?" I ask, knowing the answer is yes. I hope for stories of baby-you but get none. I think she can't remember. If you were my little girl, I'd remember.

We sit at my small round parlor table. Studying my cards, I press your leg. You press back. The game is slow. Not knowing numerals, your mother must, at first, count spots. We are not impatient. We can sit this way for any length of time. You would kiss me now, no nonsense. But you wasted our chance and we have to wait.

I will know all of the other Dowling women before the

winter is out, but I can't imagine liking any better than this one. I like her strong body for making you and her big bosom for feeding you and her hands for petting and dressing you. I suppose they swatted you too. We will forgive them, because now they are spotty and veiny, newly innocent.

The game gets easier for her. Before we stop, I have the happiness of seeing her smile. She is enjoying herself. I have made her easy in my house.

Your leaving is not unbearable. Something social rises in me and helps. I touch the back of your neck once, lightly, with my fingertip as I help you on with your jerkin. Then I kiss your cheek and hers.

"We'll read tomorrow," I say.

I think I like it better this way than I thought I could. To work and play together, to be out of bed, almost behaving ourselves, gives us something we have needed.

There has been a storm all day. This morning it woke me, howling and pelting my windows with snow and sleet. It's still going on, late afternoon, as strong as ever. Maybe stronger.

In the still-new pleasure of cozy solitude, I am sewing. How lovely to sew without a nag of guilt. (Edward has hired a girl, and I am simply Martha's neighbor now, not her servant.) I am making firpins for you, which I measured you for from memory—one hand *here* and the other *here* is how far? The firpins will be bolder than I and touch you where I have not. They will caress your body all day, as my lucky ambassador—lieutenant—proxy—and at unexpected, inconvenient times you will remember to feel their touch, which is my touch, and your heart will pound. My heart is pounding at the thought. It is the sort of problem I like for us to have.

And you are in your father's house, thinking of me, and damnation! you are thinking the storm's so bad you won't come tonight. You are thinking, in fact, that I wouldn't *want* you to come, that I don't expect you.

Now listen! Now listen here!

But you won't listen. I'm like a fly in a bottle, buzz buzz. You don't hear a thought I'm sending you. You are smug in my love and your belief that I care only for your comfort.

Oh what a maddening girl you are! You have the boots for it, the breeches, the long strong legs, everything but plain common sense and the ears to hear me.

I sigh. No use waiting till it's even darker and even harder. Sigh. Put on extra woolen stockings. Knot the tops. Put shoes back on. Sigh. Put more stockings on over the shoes. Knot the tops. Extra petticoat. Oh, unkind Sarah! You could *leap* here, on your wonderful legs. And I'll be trudging and toiling. Well. Scarf over chin and nose-end. Round and round. Shawl. Cloak. Hood up. Another scarf. Mittens. Lantern.

Trudge and toil, yes! This is an ice storm. The sky is falling. Fences are glazed, trees glazed. In short order, *I* am glazed. No traction for my glazed stockings. And now not even dim light from the sky. The tiny worthless dots my lantern sheds don't even show my feet. Toil on, poor wayfarer, buffeted, tossed, a lonely fragile bark, whose only crime is a heart too loving.

No thanks to you, I gain your door. Your worthless dogs, asleep for the winter I suppose, don't challenge me. I pound your door. No one inside can believe, of course, the testimony of mere ears. A knock on a night like this? Yes, you ninnies! I pound again. Who do you *think* it is? Who else *could* it be? Didn't I tell you, I have to see you every day? I suppose you're all huddled together in wonderment, preparing to delegate Big Ira to go see what that unaccountable noise is, that sounds so much like somebody at the door.

As I reach to pound once more, the door fades back from me and there you are. Not surprised. Your perceptions are improving. I can make you feel me through a door, even though not through a storm. One step at a time.

You are <u>miserable</u>. And you are right to be. Your whole hangdog figure drips guilt. Good.

I have friends in this house who are glad to see me even if you're not. You and your father may stand over there and shift from foot to foot and wonder what to do with me. I am nevertheless well welcomed. I kiss your mother and then on reflection your sisters too, except Rachel. She is scowling at me.

"*Read*ing lesson!" I say, and I notice that I have never before heard my voice so cheerful.

But they will not hear of reading till I am rested and warmed. Two little ones (I must remember their names: Lucy and Katy) kneel and strip my icy stockings off. They are so innocent, reaching under my skirts, intent on stocking tops, never supposing I might find them forward. And I don't. I chance a look at you while their hands explore my legs, but your father is beside you so I look into the fire and smile a very small secret smile, hardly more than a pleasant expression, which only you and he and Rachel will understand.

I should have brought paper. These girls need copybooks. They need slates. With a stick I write LUCY and KATY in the ash dust on the hearth. I write LIZZY. I write EMMA. They are in a row with their bottoms up, copying their names in the dust. I write MARY. Rachel would like her name, but not from me. She won't ask and I won't offer. She and I are very much alike. We are both in love with you. I may sympathize with her feeling and even grudgingly find a certain beauty in it, but I don't think I'm obliged to help her with it. Why should she sleep by you and I sleep alone?

I say, "Well, now, Sarah, I'm ready to hear you read."

You bring out your Garvey. I sit behind you on a stool,

following and correcting over your shoulder. You make many mistakes.

Your father says, "Not doing too good."

I am afraid he is on the verge of violating the new unwritten law, that he see nothing and suspect nothing and foremost say nothing. He's afraid of driving you away again, doesn't he know that?

Serenely I say, "She's doing very well. This isn't the book we've been using."

He subsides. We go on. I think you really can read better than this. I don't know for sure. I do my part— I do not rest my chin on your shoulder, I do not put my hands on your hips.

Your mother says, "You better stay the night."

"Oh, no, I couldn't," I say. "Anyway, the storm is moderating, I think." At which a gust full of pellets hits the house like a load of hay to make a liar out of me.

"You better stay," she says.

I look at the little ones. Their faces are very flattering to me, all these eager pretty girls doting unconcealed. I do have an effect on the Dowling women. I imagine I could even win Rachel over, in time, if I cared to. She liked me well enough the day she brought Parson Peel's letter over.

I look at you. You too want me to stay. The night could be pleasant. So much so that you might be willing to repeat it.

I say, "Thank you all the same, Mrs. Dowling. I must get home."

Their urgings continue, but I resume my not-yet-dry wraps and stockings, light my lantern, and set off. I have not exchanged a private word or a real look with you, but I hope I have told you, in a way you will believe and remember, that we will have a daily life. If you are too timid to have it beautifully, in Genesee, we will have it this way, in Connecticut.

You are angry about something. You come faithfully every evening, bringing a sister, but you do not help me to seize the little moments we might have. You do not come down cellar with me when I go for cider. You are always looking away when I try for your eye. At least, not being agitated, you show me how well you can read.

I should be trying to guess what's gone wrong, but I shall wait and let you tell me Sabbath afternoon.

And now you too understand about staying out of bed when there's something that needs to be discussed. I think I could not get you to bed today, by any ordinary means, until we talk.

You are full of your topic and not shy. Your anger makes you handsome in a way I haven't seen before.

"What made you come to my place?" you ask.

"I have to see you every day," I say. *Demurely,* I think, is how.

"Do you call that seeing?"

"I take what I can get."

You say, "I won't have it. I won't be made to do what I judge is foolish."

"No, Sarah. I have made only my own choice. Your choice is still your own. I'm not making you do anything."

"You're making me come every day."

"And you consider it foolish?"

"Some days it's foolish. In an ice storm, it's foolish."

"All right, I'll be the foolish one in nasty weather."

"You know I can't have that either."

"It's not for you to say. It's my choice. You could choose to hide away and not see me. I couldn't help that. But you can't choose whether or not I'll come. In any weather you find troublesome, look for me."

"You want me out in storms, to see you when we can't kiss or talk or anything. It's not worth it."

"To me, it is worth it. I value many things about you besides your kiss. So I'll be out in storms."

"You won't. You know I'd break my back to spare you that. Oh, I thought love would be so sweet! I thought things would go *easier!* You're running me. You're playing me. Stop playing me."

(I do have my hook in your mouth, darling, but I'm not playing you; I'm landing you. I'd better, don't you think, before we're both too old for the walk in any weather? It does no harm that you are not deceived. One should not be able to deceive a woman.)

I say, "There's another way. We can go to Genesee."

"We can't."

"Or you could live here. There's room."

I block your "no" with a kiss. "Don't say no until you think about it," I say, and then because it's been so long since we had a proper chance, I kiss you again and again, and as always when this begins we talk no more.

You come to me through the dark, when you need rest, when the snow is deep and blowing, when no sister is gracious about accompanying you, when your mother protests and your father threatens, you come to me. And now you know as well as I, that you cannot resist me. We both need the proof.

You are so much finer than I, noble, generous, devoted to freedom, unwilling to bully. But it is I, and the traits in which I differ from you, who will save us.

I love to alarm you by making my lips into a kiss when our chaperone is intent on her book. She could look up at any time, of course, and it makes the fun, watching you try to shake your head without shaking it, try to indicate her without moving. I stay reckless and imperious, not pitying your blush and your puffed-up throat, leaving it up to you whether to get us caught by leaving me there unanswered. You can always be made to answer, and then I bow my head and smile.

We even make some progress in reading. Your sisters,

too, learn easily. I am fond of them, but I begin to be sorry that they are so fond of me. Now they will be as sorry to part from me as from you.

Sometimes I wonder how much of your love for me is gratitude for the ways I have made their lives more interesting. I have made them small gifts, such as cards and jackstraws, and of course the reading, if they are able to go on with it, can give them the world. You dream, I think, of the number of times your mother may be moved to smile. I suspect you of wanting to spend not only your own life but mine in adding to their pleasures. If I would let you, you would be happy to consider our love the weekly refreshment we need for going on with this main task.

As a teacher I groan for your wasted family, but as a woman I must choose only one of you to be devoted to.

Perhaps you are too young. At twenty-two, would I have left everything for love, as I ask you to? Even last year, at twenty-seven (to remember what I would rather forget), I couldn't go with you. But you are better than I. Everything depends on your being better than I. You have nothing to learn. You need only to be guided to recover what you always knew.

We are lying together on my winter bed in the kitchen, in a sweet afterwards.

"Stay by me. Live here," I say.

"You said to think on it, so I did. I think you don't need me here and my folks do."

"Not need you! I need your warm body in bed and your—I *need* you."

"Not my work. You don't need that. And the folks do. Here I'd just be your pet, and get in your brother's hair."

I say, "Do you want another winter like this one?"

"Yes!"

"Exactly like this one?"

You bite your lip and pretend to think. "I'd settle," you say.

"Do you want ten more exactly like this one?"

"I'd settle."

"How about twenty-five? Fifty? We can live to be eighty. Who's to say we won't? Old maids often do."

"I hope we do."

"You hope to be tottering across the ice on your rickety brittle old bones every night of your seventy-fourth winter? Which will be my eightieth winter?"

Your eyes are so bright, laughing and unimpressed. You get up and creak around the room, to show me age seventy-four as it is usually experienced, and then leap to show the form it will take in you. I am rebuked that I believe in death. It is our whole difference, I see now. Believing in death has made me brave. It could do the same for you, but maybe there's no hurry. You charm me so, just as you are. Leap, leap you go, holding your skirt up to show me your legs. In lax and heathen York State, surely we can dance? You land so lightly in your soft blue stockings, washed and darned a thousand times. I love you.

In an old cracked voice you say, "Patience? Pate? Patty?" and peer for me everywhere and see me and become young and bound towards me. I curl up laughing, for I suspect that you intend to tickle me. You pry my body straight and lie on it and kiss me. "*Just* like this, I'll settle," you say.

It may take years. It may take age twenty-eight, to believe in death. I decide to enjoy the six years. I reach up and hold your face, luring you into a kiss. You are in no hurry. You like it up there, looking at me, making me wait. Before it can go to your head I pull you down and we join our mouths together in a seal I am willing to make permanent and then someone says, "*What* are you doing?" not gentle or in sympathy or in any way that belongs in the same room with love, and I consider who might be capable of such an offense.

Who but Martha?

You pull up from me and stand, oh greatly agitated. I almost think you may run out without your shoes or wraps. I sit up and take your hand. "Settle down, darling," I say.

You look at me wildly. I smile. "It's nothing," I say. And then you're not afraid either. You are not a coward. You are only afraid that I am. I am so relieved that I am not, just as I hoped not to be.

Martha stares a while. I don't suppose she wants an answer. I don't suppose there can be any need to ask of two people with disarrayed hair and opened bodices who are lying in bed and kissing so deeply they can't hear someone come in, what are you doing? I stand beside you, holding your hand, and wait for her to go away. She does, and then I neaten your clothes and hair, and mine, and neaten the bed, and tug the rope that lifts it back to the ceiling. Edward will be along.

He pounds the door vigorously and waits until I call, "Come in." His wife should take up the custom. Perhaps she will in the future. He never has before. It is not the country way. My poor brother. He would like very much to see our embrace, and so he concludes he mustn't.

But I don't despise his decency and honor. I rely on them.

You are on the bench, looking into the fire. I am at the wheel. He goes to the window and looks at it. It is too frosty to look through. We say nothing. I will not be forward and unwomanly and set him against us. I meekly wait. He clears his throat, and then clears it again.

"I hoped all this was done with," he says.

I say nothing, and of course you don't.

He says, "Have you prayed to be freed of it?"

I say, "I meant to. Last summer I got as far as my

knees." (You turn and stare at me. Well, darling, of course there are some things about me you don't know.)

"But didn't pray?" he asks.

"I found I didn't wish to be freed of it."

Gravely he says, "The Devil wouldn't let you pray."

"I prayed. But not for that. I prayed to be fulfilled in it."

He thinks it over. It is impressive that God didn't strike me with lightning for such a prayer. There is a chance that God is not offended.

I must leave everything for Edward to think of. I wait.

"Martha's upset," he says.

I say, "I'm sorry."

"She says she hoo-hooed pretty loud and you didn't hear."

I bow my head.

She says it could've been anybody. One of the children. A neighbor. It's God's blessing she was the one."

"Yes."

"She feels you must be made to stop. Can you tell me you will try?"

I am silent.

He says, "She wasn't told about the other time."

"Thank you."

"So she thinks it's still a bud that can be nipped."

Now there is a long silence.

He says, "I won't be rushed. I need time to think this through. Martha can't make up my mind for me. I have to meditate and pray."

"I'll do the same," I say.

"Good day, Miss Dowling," he says, looking at you for the first time. He is taking your measure. Your worth is clear to see. I trust he sees it. In any case, he likes you.

"Mr. White," you say shyly, and nod.

He goes. I sit beside you on the bench. You put your arm around me. I lean against your side.

"What do you think he'll do?" you ask.

"I think he'll ask me to leave. I needn't, though. I am protected by my father's will. We needn't go until you want to."

"If we don't go, then he'll do something else. Like keep me away. Should I come tomorrow?"

"Of course. We won't stop anything we can still do."

"Patty?" you say. "Patty, did you know Martha was going to come in?"

"No. But I knew someday somebody would."

Martha and I meet in the barn. It is early morning. She sits at her cow and I at mine. The milk hisses into our pails. She wants to remark but can't decide how to begin. I won't help her.

"I always knew there was something wrong with you," she says. That needn't have taken so much thought. She could have blurted that out first thing. "Many times I've tried to make Edward see it, but no."

"He wouldn't see?" I ask, pleased.

"Oh, no! Not *his* sister! Nothing could be wrong with *his* sister! How many times I said it, 'Edward, she means to make you keep her all her life. She means not to marry and do her part,' and he'd just say, 'Oh, she's young yet.' Young!"

"Good Edward," I say.

"Well, now he's got to see. Spoiled and indulged like a princess! And see what comes of it. If I had my way you'd soon be glad to marry like any other woman, and not too fussy who, and do your part. Nothing but spoiled. What made you think you needn't marry except pure spoiled? And think you could do things man and wife don't do?"

"Kiss? Don't you kiss?" I am very curious. I have had no such confidences before. To skirt so close to someone else's secret life! Yes. I am curious.

"I won't say," she says. With stool and pail she flounces to her next cow. "Not like that we don't. I wouldn't care to. Not like that."

I say, "Well, of course, if you wouldn't care to—"

"I wasn't brought up that way."

(But I wasn't either.)

She says, "Wait till I tell Edward how you've been this morning. Cool as a pirate, not an ounce of decent shame in you. It's a *sin,* you know. I don't expect Edward remembered to mention that to you. Saint Paul forbids it."

"He does?"

"With all your Bible reading and Bible pictures, you don't know that? And your fronts all open like no-good Jezebels, and not caring who might walk in and find you, and *her not even in the family!*"

I am astonished. "Martha—Sister—" I begin, but I am too astonished to go on. And perhaps she doesn't realize what she has said.

It is afternoon. I am at my table, painting Saul on the road to Damascus. There's a tap at my door and then I hear it open. That will be Martha with her Bible.

She sits down half around the table from me. "I had some trouble finding the passage," she says. "It's not one I expected to have a need for."

I say, "You see, you put my mind on Paul. Here comes Saul, the raging wolf with all his attendants, who will all be wolfish too—perhaps you can't tell at this stage. But, see, the road bends, and we can see, although Saul can't, that in just about one minute he will be knocked flat by love and rise up Saint Paul."

"I expect you want to claim that's what happened to you."

"No."

"Well, don't, because here's what he says," and Martha reads in her false flat reading voice: " 'Wherefore God also gave them up to uncleanness through the lusts of their own hearts, to dishonor their own bodies between themselves: who changed the truth of God into a lie, and worshipped and served the creature more than the Creator, who is blessed forever. Amen. For this cause God gave them up unto vile affections: for even their women did change the natural use into that which is against nature: And likewise also the men, leaving the natural use of the women, burned in their lust toward one another; men with men working that which is unseemly, and receiving in themselves that recompence of their error which was meet. And even as they did not like to retain God in their knowledge, God gave them over to a reprobate mind, to do those things which are not convenient; being filled with all unrighteousness, covetousness, maliciousness; full of envy, murder, debate, deceit, malignity; whisperers, backbiters, haters of God, despiteful, proud, boasters, inventors of evil things, disobedient to parents, without understanding, covenantbreakers, without natural affection, implacable, unmerciful: who knowing the judgment of God, that they which commit such things are worthy of death, not only do the same, but have pleasure in them that do them. Therefore thou art inexcusable, O man, whosoever thou art that judgest; for wherein thou judgest another, thou condemnest thyself; for thou that judgest doest the same things.' "

Martha doesn't like the drift of the last part, so she stops there.

The condemnation is powerful indeed. I cannot answer it. I must bear it. May God save my heart for love, despite Saint Paul.

"I see you thought you could argue it away, but you can't," Martha says.

"No. He says it. He says I am worthy of death. So be it."

I continue to paint. She watches against her will. Everybody likes to see a painter at work. She needn't be ashamed.

Since I cannot dispute Saint Paul, we sit in silence. My house smells good, from a cake I am baking for you. It is snug here and pretty and quiet and fragrant. Martha is bothered by the seductions of my house. She starts to go, but doesn't. Close by my side, alarmingly close, she lingers and says, "It could've been so sweet, working and helping each other here. It was what I thought about. It was what I thought would be. Edward and you and me together. And then you didn't like me anymore, and I forgot I liked you, and I just lately remembered. Do you remember we used to like each other?"

Keeping such distance as I can, I say, "Yes."

"I get so lonesome with just Edward. We don't kiss. There's something he does to me, but we don't kiss. We're not sweet together. And the children. And the girl. She's no better than you were, Patience. She's sullen too. So many times I wish I could sit by you of an evening, but I expect you wouldn't want that."

How cruel and cold to leave her there, unhugged, unreceived. But she's too late. I am yours now, and my hugs are only yours.

She says, "No, you wouldn't." (Her voice hard again.) "You've got those Dowlings trooping in here every night, and them not even in the family."

She and her Bible go. I am uneasy. What would Saul have done if love had flung him down and then decided not to keep him after all?

Edward has finished two days of meditation and prayer. He is here to tell me my fate. I sit with my hands folded, meekly ready to accept it, in case it is a fate I am willing to accept.

"You have made a great mistake," he begins. "These are the passions marriage is meant to discourage and then extinguish. At first we imagine and hope, but in marriage we learn we are not wanted. But we find solace in work and in making the world go. I speak of men. I have no idea what women feel or want. Have you?"

"No. Not in general."

"Most people manage well enough with marriage and work, but what's to become of you? You have wakened feelings marriage can't help you with. You let them wake, and you let them grow, and you took pleasure in thinking of them, and here we are. As to work, I honestly don't see how a woman's work uses her mind enough to help her this way. She can't fight these feelings by work. The only hope is not to let them wake."

"But here we are," I say, quite timidly. I do, in fact, feel timid. I have taken a terrible risk. His power is very real. I am grateful to Martha for telling me that he cares more for me than he ever seemed to. Except for knowing this, I might not be able to bear the frights of this confrontation.

"Yes, here we are. You've made us all a problem. And I have had to think what it is my duty to do about it."

"Have you decided?"

"I considered all the things I might do," he says. "First was the possibility of turning my back on it all and letting it go on. But Martha found you, and someday the children could, or a neighbor, and then the family is disgraced and the children unmarriageable. I confess I couldn't be quite blind. I turned my back all this while, I confess, and here we are."

"Yes."

"Next was asking the girl's father to keep her away, as he did before. It would mean brute force, considering the feelings you've encouraged in each other. It would be difficult, but duty often is. It's what Martha wants."

Oh praise God for Martha! Except that she wants this, it is what he would do.

He says, "I think the end of such a course would be that I had to declare you mad, and build you a cage in the loft."

I am shocked. I haven't thought of this at all.

"But I'm not mad," I say.

"No. But you soon would be."

"Yes."

"And there's grounds to question that it would be best to drive you mad. It's a blot on a family, madness. I think it's not my duty to bring it on."

"I hope not," I choke.

"You spoke last year of wanting to go to Genesee."

To hide my relief and pleasure—because I don't want him to think that he is shirking the duty of punishing me —I say, "That has come to seem unreasonable."

"I thought so at the time."

"Yes, I know you did."

"It's the only solution I see now. It needn't be to Genesee, of course. But I can't let you stay here."

"Our father's will—" I say, knowing Edward must have thought of it. I don't want to think of an objection he hasn't anticipated and dismissed.

"I am prepared to make a money settlement for your property here."

"But then my subsistence. Who can say how much it might be worth over the years?"

"Woman! Are you trying to drive a hard bargain? You are in no position to." He frowns magnificently. We are a handsome family. I hope that God will someday give Edward, too, the great task he longs for. "You can trust me to be fair."

"I know I can, Edward. When must I go?"

"You are not helpless. You are in good health, and you know how to do all the female things, and how to keep school."

"Yes. When must I go?"

"And she'll be with you, I assume. At least there can be no children. The two of you alone can manage, if you'll go where land is cheap and the arts you know are wanted."

"How soon?" I say.

"The sin is for your own soul to bear. I've done what I can if I protect my family."

What can I say to reassure him that he is being harsh enough?

I try. "To leave the home my father built me! The protection of my brother! His children! My friends!" To say it is to see some truth in it. My tears are quite unexpected and unforced, almost guileless.

"You might have thought of that before," he says, feeling better.

"Couldn't Sarah just live here with me?" He can tell Martha that I begged for that, but that he was strong and cruel.

"I'm not obliged to keep her in food and shoes, to let her be an example to my daughters."

I submit and say no more, but think sad true thoughts to bring the tears along.

He says, "There's a parcel of land I can turn into money. I'll have it soon."

"It's winter!" I say.

"If you want to make a crop this year, you should be starting. It won't be long. Can you behave yourself, knowing it won't be long? There can be no more in this house."

I nod.

"Tell me there will be no more in this house. I know your nods."

"There will be no more in this house." I'm afraid it will be easy to keep this promise. I pray that my feeling can flow again when we have built our private place.

He says, "I'll draw up papers. You can't squander your birthright and then come back. Don't expect to."

"No."

"You'll need a map. I can spare you one."

"Thank you."

He pushes back his chair and gets up. At the door he turns and says, "Would you really rather go than give her up?"

I risk the truth. "Yes, Edward."

He shakes his head. "So be it," he says, and opens the door to go. Again he turns. "But what do you *do?*" he asks.

My maidenly blush calls forth in him a manly blush. He does not stay for answer.

I must see you. There is no time to lose. I am flinging on my cloak to go to you, when I notice that it is almost evening already. You will soon be here, perhaps before I can get my milking done.

No matter who comes with you, I will speak.

You bring the one I would have chosen, your mother. She is not awkward now, knowing my affection for her. I take her hand and lead her to the fireside. You must make your own way.

"I have news," I say.

Your mother says, "I hope good."

"I'll tell it, and let you decide which. I'm going to the west." I feel you start and tighten.

She says, "Oh! When?" and although she must have had some idea she has to stop and blow her nose and look away.

"It could be as little as a week. Whenever my brother gets my money for me."

"Oh. In such weather?"

"It's none too early. I have a long way to go and I want to buy land and get a start this year."

"It's a chancey step," she says.

"Yes, it is. But I've wanted it for a long time. Last summer when I kept school, I made up stories for the children about the frontier, when I was supposed to be reading them the Bible."

She smiles weakly. "I'll miss you. We all will."

"I want to take Sarah with me."

"I figured."

"I knew you did."

I turn to you. "Will you?"

You stride around my kitchen. "Going's a different thing to making up stories," you say. "You got no more idea than a jaybird," you say. "Just when I can be some good here," you say.

You keep on pacing. Your mother and I wait.

You say, "I want to. But is that any reason? When I can be some good here finally?"

You mean, is it right to choose pleasure over duty? Can you yield to a longing for kisses, when other people's necessities are at stake? Nothing you ever heard of tells you you have a right to choose me. I hoped you'd thought this through before. I may have to go without you. There may not be time, before, for you to face and learn to endure your own necessities. When I am gone you will, and then I will send for you.

"I'll be going anyway," I say, to let you know that I am being compelled to go. "First will you do something for me?"

"Anything!"

"Stand still and let me measure you. I have a length of goods I can't look at without thinking of your hair."

"Oh, no!"

"You said, 'Anything.'"

You press your lips together, a stubborn child, but I will not let you off. What are you to travel in if I do? I bring my measure and make you stand. Your mother keeps the notes. She draws numerals very nicely now. I suppose she's been practicing in the hearth dust.

(You see, sweetheart, it's not so bad to be measured when I do it.)

"What'll Pa say about me living off of him all winter and then leaving again as spring comes on?"

Your mother says, "He'll say nothing."

I see a new Mrs. Dowling. Women are not so very powerless after all. He will say nothing. She should make up her mind more often.

CHAPTER TWO

Here we go. It is cold clear dawn, a March morning. There may be bare dirt for Edward to bring his sleigh back over, but it slips along easily now. We are nested together in a little row, Edward and then me and then you, under bearskin robes. He is seeing us off in style, probably in the thought that it's a blot on a family, too, to let a member leave under what could be interpreted as a cloud.

Your whole side is pressed against mine. There wouldn't be room between us for a thread. Your face is very sad, and mine must be too—we've both been weeping. Although I think it shows no dislike of what we go to, to feel a grief for what we leave, I want to comfort you. I slide my hand under the robe, hoping you will do the same so I can reach you in hiding there. Either you don't understand or you decide against it.

The horses clip along, carrying us into parts I haven't seen since my father brought me home at the end of my education. I leave my country without having looked at it or known it, as someday I must leave the world. Uncheerful thoughts like this assail me, but the harness bells are as merry as a wedding party.

Yes. A wedding party. Of course. I uncover my hand and in the open, under the sky, under the eyes of my brother, I reach for your hand inside the muff I gave you. Surprise makes you start and almost draw back, but then you accept me. We ride now palm to palm. I marry you. Embracing inside secret walls never married us. The open, the sky, the eyes of my brother marry us and the harness bells are our wedding hymn.

There is no pleasure in it. Is there usually, in a wedding? The object is a public declaration, and an earnest of intent to build private joy again.

Edward says nothing. We all sit staring straight ahead, like figureheads. After some miles I feel sufficiently declared, and squeeze your hand, and let it fall.

Earnest of intent is what I have from Edward: enough money to journey comfortably by ship and coach. I have also his promise that when we find the farm we want he will send the means to hold it, and every year thereafter enough to make the payments, until I have received a total of one thousand dollars. I don't know whether this is generous or not, in exchange for my part of my father's house and my cows, and all the things I couldn't cram into three trunks, and a lifetime's keep. I just don't have any way of knowing. It depends on what a lifetime's keep might have come to.

I have sworn that I will ask no more, and not come back again. Our agreement is all written up, signed and sealed, witnessed by upright witnesses. The Supreme Court could not set it aside. Yet all that gives it value is that Edward is honorable, and I am. If he should fail me, could I come back and law with him, without a cent to pay a lawyer? And if I should fall on evil days and present myself helpless at his door, could he turn me away? We might have left all to honor in the first place, as you and I, without a marriage contract, leave all to love.

The coastal trader is due today, in its own haphazard way. It may have been and gone already. It may come tomorrow. Against my will, I get a feeling that if we have not missed it, and if it comes today, our whole journey will go well. I do not like omens so weighted against me, but it is what was sent.

We reach Stratford midmorning. From afar we see masts, and then our lovely ragamuffin ship, wide, ungraceful, low in the water, so beautiful. I choke with relief at the sight of it.

We are far from late. The captain is auctioning the cargo he got upcoast, which is barrels of oil and rum, salted fish, and cloth and dyestuffs and glass. He stands on a bale, hammering and chanting. He is bartering for Stratford horses and cheese and butter. I like to think that some of the cheeses are mine.

Mockingly, Edward says, "I except you want to start fending for yourselves now?"

Immediately you climb out, but I catch your arm and whisper, "I have all of our money. Stay here. I'll go." Then I climb out, and while I am considering how to move through this crowd of men and horses and interrupt this busy captain and hire him to carry us to New-York, Edward gestures us both back and goes himself. We wait beside the sleigh like shy children.

We look at each other and smile for each other's sakes.

"We'll be all right," I say.

"Yes," you say doubtfully.

"I have a way of knowing. Were you afraid when you set off before?"

"No, but then it was just me and I didn't care."

Edward returns. "It's taken care of," he says. "Come on."

You hand me your muff and start to lift one of the trunks. Even to me the sight is odd, and Edward is shocked. "No, no!" he says. "I'll get a boy. Come on board."

Stubbornly you keep your hands on the trunk. "I got to begin," you say.

I say, "Later, not now," so you yield and Edward makes a way for us across the dock and up the gangplank.

It is best not to be two women alone on such a walk. He establishes us on splintery benches inside the ship where we can't see anything, the Ladies' Cabin. He goes back to see to our baggage. The captain is chanting again, recovered from the flurry of our arrival. The crewmen with many curses are loading horses. I do see we mustn't go outside while men are cursing.

We sit close together. Maidenly shyness can seem to be the reason, if anyone sees us. Indeed, it may be the real reason. There is no excitement in pressing against your side.

You say, "I been worried about what all I can't do to take care of you. I *know* I'm not strong's a man. I'm not such a fool as I was. But now not to be let to do even what I can! I could've toted the trunks easy. If you're wanting me to be a lady, I don't see how it's to go."

"Just until we get away from Edward," I say. "He's been good to us. Just a little longer, for his sake."

Even I can hear my tinniness, so how can you miss it? The fact is, you are right. There will be these issues all along our way, and I will be ruled by this folly: I do want you to be a lady around other people, even though it's because you are not a lady that there is hope for us.

You say, "Then when we get to New-York I'm to take the trunks off?" and you smile unhappily, knowing better.

I say, "It does seem to matter to me. I know it's nonsense. It will probably pass quite soon since I do know it's nonsense. Can you be patient with me?"

The worry briefly leaves your face while you look at me tenderly. Yes, you will be patient with me, and I in turn will hurry.

Now you are restless again, fidgety. You get up and pace around our small dim dingy enclosure. I admire your princely stride, the flow of the almond-dyed wool dress I made you, your strength, your stubborn beauty. May God make me worthy of you, in a hurry.

Edward returns. Our baggage is stowed aboard, he says, and our passage paid, and no I needn't bother about what it cost him.

"Thank you, Edward," I say, standing. A formal moment: we shall not meet again.

"Take care," he says. "Do your part. Write to me. Work hard. I wish you happiness."

"You *do?*" I say, amazed and touched to tears. "Oh, Brother, if you do—if you really do—give us your blessing on our day of beginning!"

"With all my heart," he says.

I am weeping and he puts his arms around me. I am engulfed in the male scratchiness and smell of his coat. He says, "Of course I give my blessing. I took for granted you'd know that. Little pesky bullhead sister! Of course I hope you find the life you were born for. It wasn't here. I hope it's there. I have cared for you. Of course."

Now you come near and he hugs us both in the same hug. He looks at you, so kindly. "I wouldn't want, myself, to let too much depend on how long a woman's love lasts," he says. "But—take care of her—don't let her run you—God keep you."

He kisses my cheek and then yours and then mine again, and then he goes without looking back.

I can't remember one single thing I don't like about my brother Edward.

BOOK FOUR

Sarah

CHAPTER ONE

I said, "He had no call to say that to me."

"What? What did he say?"

Then I remembered something Parson told me, how you must never say a word against somebody's wife or husband or house or child or brother or sister, and if *they* say something, contradict them.

"Nothing," I said, and Patience sat there looking sappy and overcome because Edward liked her after all, like it was a wonder she didn't deserve. To my mind, he was too fond, not just of her but of me too, and I suspect he liked to think about us. I wouldn't begrudge him that, exactly, except he put on such holy airs.

The anchor chain came rumbling up, and considering what interesting things the sailors would start doing I asked Patience, "Would you like to go up and watch?"

"No," she said. "I want to think." I figured it was likely her brother she had to keep marveling over, so I left her there and went up by myself.

And it was a sight, how the sails unwrinkled and caught the wind and the dock slipped away and the town. I began to not want to see it after all, though, with Patience missing it, so I went back down the steep little stairway and started through the little passage.

There was a finely dressed man there that I couldn't easy

get past. He was friendly and real smiley glad to see me so I smiled too and said, "I been up above seeing how they run this thing," and he said, "Are you alone?" and I said, "Oh, no, I'm with a lady." He said, "Perhaps we'll meet in New-York," and to be polite I said, "Perhaps," and then he crowded over against the wall to let me past and I started past and when I was between him and the other wall, he grabbed me.

Well, there wasn't room enough in that little narrow passage to use any of what I knew about fighting and making a throw and all that and anyway he had my arms pinned. I said, but not loud (I would've been ashamed to be found like that), "Let me go. Let me go," and he said I liked him, he knew I did, and why should I play I didn't? I said I didn't like him, and I upped with my knee to knee him but I missed because he bent away and it only made him laugh and ask where I learned *that* little trick? And would I really do harm to the Lady's Best Friend he had inside there? He said he liked a fish that fought and he wouldn't let it interfere with our friendship that I didn't agree right away with him on every detail. He said when I came to my senses he'd give me his card so I'd know where to find him whenever I could get away from my mistress.

I thought somehow he knew that Patience was my lover, because that's a word, mistress, that's used for that, I think, and it made me kind of weak and nervous, *shocked* to tell the truth, so I stopped struggling for a little second and he thought he had me so he eased off a little. I nearly broke away, but he got a new hold on me, and I began to think I'd have to do all I could. But I didn't *want* to break his foot or bite his throat, and while I was studying if I might have to, I heard Patience say, very cold and furious, "Let her go."

Which, just like that, he did, and he picked up his hat so he could have it to take off for Patience, and he bowed but she was giving him a glare I'd've died if she ever gave me, and he felt it too, though not the same, naturally.

She touched me to send me ahead of her along the passage. I heard her coming along behind me. "You'd better keep an eye on that one, ma'am," he called. "You notice she wasn't calling for help, ma'am."

She didn't answer him. I heard her coming along behind me, not fast or slow. I wanted to go fast, myself, but I didn't want to leave her alone with that man either, even though I kind of knew he wouldn't lay a hand on *her*. It shamed and scared me clear to my shoe soles to think there was something about me that made him think he could do to me like he did. I don't see how I could've felt much worse if he'd out-and-out humped me, I felt that much soiled, but the worst was feeling I'd brought it on myself somehow.

Then I thought of something worse yet, which was that *Patience* would think I'd brought it on, and think I was soiled. By the time we had the door of the Ladies' Cabin shut behind us, I was so choked up and dry in the mouth and nervous in the stomach I thought I might fall down.

She stood with her back against the door. I couldn't look at her. I sat down on the bench and put my hands over my face.

"Did he hurt you, angel?" she asked.

I never heard a word so beautiful as that "angel" right then, but my voice shook anyway when I said, "No."

"If he did, I'll kill him," she said, so quiet.

"He didn't hurt me. Just my pride."

She knelt and took my wrists but didn't pull my hands down. She said, "Are you weeping?"

"No. I'm blushing."

"Oh, I will, I'll kill him. I'll buy a gun and blow his foul head off." Then she called me words like innocent and pure and her lamb and her treasure, that sounded so sweet coming at a time when I needed them so much.

She stood up beside me and held my head snug against

her front. I felt her hand under my chin and let her tip
my face up.

"Did he kiss you?"

"No."

There was so much pain in her face I almost couldn't
look at her, and then I saw coming over her the feeling
we'd had before but hadn't had for weeks lately, from
worrying and being watched and being scorned and all,
and from her promising her brother we wouldn't in his
house. I felt she could kiss me again the way she used
to, except this would be fiercer and not careful about
anything and how could it stop and what would become
of us? I bowed my head.

She said, "Kiss me!" but luckily I didn't want to right
then. If we'd both felt the same, I just don't know what.

I stood up, saying, "Not yet. Not here," and I walked
around. I felt almost all right, to think that Patience had
her feeling back. I always knew my own feeling would
come back, but I did have some little doubt about hers
until right then. How it turned out, my doubt was foolish,
but who could've said ahead of time we wouldn't just be
friends and partners the rest of our time together and
never have our glory again? Once your heart's gone dead
from being scorned, nobody can say for sure it will ever
grow back. Maybe it was mean-spirited to walk around
feeling better when Patience was still getting herself in
hand about the kiss she couldn't have, but it's what I
did.

I also felt comforted to know she'd take my part even
when I wasn't entirely in the right. Then I thought maybe
she didn't realize I wasn't, and I felt obliged to say,
"Maybe something I did made him think—a fine-dressed
gentleman like that."

"He's a scoundrel and a rascal and a stinking lout and
a monster!" She stopped and then said, "What did you
do?"

So I told her everything that happened except I couldn't

stand to tell how he called her my mistress. But everything I did myself, I told, and from how hard it was to
tell some parts I could see for myself where I gave him
ideas. Patience didn't even have to say. I was afraid she
would anyway, but she didn't.

I looked at her face to see if she was still on my side.
She had a new expression, like she couldn't decide if I
was mostly hopeless or mostly dear. The way her eyebrows peaked together in worry seemed to say hopeless,
but her eyes said dear, and her little shut-mouth smile
and her hand holding mine said the same. I figured the
verdict was mostly dear.

She said, "I shouldn't have let you go alone."

I said, "I hope we're not to tag each other every step
the rest of our life!"

"No. Just when there are men about, and no other
women."

I said, "But I talked to men all my life. I like men. They
know what's going on. They told me about Genesee."

"In our country, they all knew you had a huge father
strong enough to strangle a bear. We're not in our country
now."

"But last summer I wasn't either, and nobody bothered
me like that."

"Last summer you were a boy," she said.

Then I remembered how Parson sort of bothered me
like that, a little bit, not really the same. I thought it was
no time to tell Patience so, in case it made her hate him
too, right when I was looking forward to getting a look
at him again soon.

She looked very worried and in a little while she said,
"It may be that one must be a male, or be owned by one,
not to be their natural victim." She sighed, so sad. "It may
be that there's no place on earth for women who refuse to
bend their necks to be the wards of males—neatly trans-
ferred from father to brother to husband to son to grave."

I never said that so fancy, but it was what I was trying

to tell her when I wanted to stay on like before. Still, now we'd started I didn't want to go back, and I didn't want her thinking like that now. The time for thoughts like that was past.

"I may hate men," she said, sort of surprised at herself.

But I remembered Parson was a man, and Edward White maybe didn't have the warmest heart but he wouldn't jump on somebody in a passageway either. I pinned Patience down to admit she didn't hate them all, but just that one. And we agreed about him.

"I despise him," she said.

I said, "He took his hat off to you."

"Which had fallen off in his struggle with you! Oh, I may kill him after all!"

I had an idea. "No, Patience, listen!" I said. "Don't you see, it was *me*. He thought he could, somehow. But you he took his hat off to. Because you're a lady and I'm not."

"I'm not a lady. I'm an ordinary country woman. I milked my cows. I forked away their dung. I helped in the fields at harvest."

"No, you're different. Didn't everybody say so? And when I come back last fall, everybody sounded strange to me, how they talked, but you. Because you talk like Parson and them. I'm used to it now, but then I could hear it."

She smiled a little. "So there's a use at last for what Miss Amelia taught me. Scoundrels tip their hats."

"Well, wouldn't you druther?"

"I druther be like you—"

"Do I sound like *that?*"

"—and have no difference made between us."

"Well, that's what I mean. *Teach* me!"

She said, "I can't. I love you the way you are. I can't bear to—imply—that you need to be—brought *up*—to some—false—I can't, Sarah. It would destroy our love."

I said, "Why honey, I know my worth. I'd never dast've

courted you unless I did. I don't say how I am is lower.
It just gets me in trouble out here. There's ways I need to
know, like I needed reading, and it don't mean you think
you're a princess if you show me."

I *know* how short a time ago I was moping because she
wouldn't let me carry the trunks. It shows how deep that
man scared me, how fast I changed my tune.

She said, "I'll tell you what. You stay here and I'll go
up on deck, and if I can get back without being indecently
approached, I'll teach you all Miss Amelia taught me."

"I don't want you up there alone!" I said. "I won't let
you! Just teach me. In time for New-York."

She smiled, and I could see I'd more or less been led.
She never meant to go up on deck, and I think she really
did hope all along to change my out-in-public manners,
but tricks that come from sparing my feelings I can't get
much upset at.

Later Parson asked about the trip, if we got scared in
Hell Gate and like that, and we had to admit we didn't
really notice Hell Gate or anything else much. We just
stayed in that mean little Ladies' Cabin and worked
on me. We'd feel the ship stop along the way, and hear
the captain auctioning again, but we never went up to
look.

I've regretted since the fine sights we missed, but I'm
just as glad we didn't know about Hell Gate till it was
passed. To think how Patience might've sunk, bound round
with gold like that! And nothing, nothing I could do to
hold her up. I shake even now, to think.

As to fixing me up, Patience didn't rightly know where
to start. She had me stand up in front of her while she
looked me over and thought. I couldn't've felt more foolish
than I did standing there like a big gawk, and I might've
called the whole thing off except I remembered it might
be the secret of how to move safe in the world without a
man.

She decided to make the first thing be, to stand there. Just stand there, with my arms hanging down and my hands folded loose together in front, which meant no fidgeting and no putting my foot up on the bench and no feeling around for pockets to rest my hands in.

"Feet closer together. Closer still. That's right," she said. "No, don't look at me. Just gaze—*idly*. Into space. See nothing. Unfocus your eyes. That's pretty good. Now stay that way."

"How long?" I asked, without moving my lips.

"That's *good!* No, don't move. I mean, it's good you already know how to talk without moving your lips. It's an essential lady skill. It's for talking about someone who is in the room. I'll tell you when to move."

It was so hard. I remembered seeing ladies everywhere standing that way at stores and outside of churches and all around, and I wondered why I never thought before how hard it might be. I was tireder after a few minutes of it than after a day's work. When Patience let me stop I just plunked myself down beside her.

She said, "While you're resting, you can practice not hearing. Now, gaze idly. See nothing. 'Well, little lady, what's a pretty little thing like you doing so far from home?' "

I stared at her.

"No, no! Don't *hear*. 'I like the little one myself.' 'No, she's a mite on the plump side for my taste. And red-headed—that's a mean disposition every time—and look at those beady little mud-colored eyes!' Stop laughing. This is serious."

I pulled myself together. It was serious.

" 'Well, are you all alone, my pretty one? Perhaps we'll meet in New-York.' Stop blushing! Don't hear. Just keep your chin level and look away. Don't see, don't hear, don't blush, it's very simple. Please, darling, try."

"Make up something different."

" 'It's surely been pleasant for March. I don't recall a

March so pleasant. Have you come far? And where are you bound? All alone? Are you and that other lady together? Are you sisters? Are you kin at all? Is anyone meeting you? Perhaps I could be of assistance? Why, ma'am, I don't believe you heard a word I said.' Good girl. And just for that you get a kiss. Yo, Sarah! It's me. You get a kiss."

"I didn't hear a word you said."

I gave her a little peck, though, and little as it was it made her nose flare. It kind of helped out my pride, to be the one to stop. I felt so sensible, and like she was just a foolish tot I had to watch over. It evened us up. One knew one thing, one another thing.

I said, "How about how I talk?"

"I like it. I love it."

"Talk sense. It's not like you nor Parson. Show me your way."

"Honey?" She looked downright guilty. "Would you mind—very much—just letting me do the talking?"

"What!"

"I mean, of course, to other people? For now?"

"Well, can't you just fix me? There shouldn't be too much left to fix. I got a start with Parson. It shouldn't take long."

"Longer than one day, I'm afraid. And do I want to? Can't you just not see and not hear and—not speak? For now?"

I thought she was being lazy, or maybe she thought I was too thick-skulled, and I made her start right there on the ship trying to get it through my head about was and were, and saw and seen, and went and have gone, and like and as, and not leaving the g's off the ends of words, on and on until my head just whirled and I agreed it might take a while. I agreed to keep my mouth shut and glad to.

The main thing left was my walk. What she wanted of me on that was no fit thing for an able-bodied full-grown person with a place to get to, but she talked me into trying. Only place to work on it was right there in that little cabin, and I could get from corner to corner across it in four steps without even stretching. Patience said we had to find a way to slow me down and shorten my step and she dug around in her pretty silk handsack for something to put on my head like Miss Amelia put books on her girls.

There was a shawl Patience was knitting in the handsack, and it got in the way of finding anything suitable. Anyway that's the excuse I made her. Why else would she pick a thing so rolly and slippery as a knitting needle? And expect me to keep it steady on my head? She wouldn't've thought she could do it herself. I doubt Miss Amelia could've, even in her prime, unless she was lucky enough to have a crease in the top of her head.

Besides the treacherous nature of the knitting needle, there was the unsteadiness of the floor tipping one way and another. Just sitting on the bench I'd lose the needle. I do think Patience made a poor choice.

She said, "Well, the main value of it is to teach erect posture, which you have already." And she praised how I hold my shoulders and head, which I mention because I wouldn't want it thought I couldn't carry myself at all.

She had me walk back and forth between the corners, and when I was taking six steps where four would've been plenty, she said, "It will have to do. Just be haughty."

Maybe I didn't do my best to mend my walk. Leastwise it never did get mended, not that day on the ship and not ever. It could be said a bigger try might've changed me, but *hopeless* is what I think.

Someone, a sailor I expect, rapped the door and called, "New-York, ladies," and I went weak. Patience said, "You are a very rich, very ill-tempered fifty-year-old lady who has always had her own way in everything. You do as you please, and you walk like a lord, and you are deaf."

We put our wraps on and gathered up our things. Our bonnet brims touched and made a little dark tunnel for a kiss.

She said, "You are very handsome and willful and eccentric and you never speak. You see no one worth speaking to. Your faithful companion, however, speaks."

We went up on deck and stood apart from the crowd of men. The sun was just setting, just about the prettiest sunset ever. It seemed like special for us, because it was our day of beginning. It seemed like nature was trying to give us its prettiest thing, because it liked us.

The river was all jammed up with ships, more than seemed right, and along the edge of the city the masts bunched up as thick as grass. I didn't see how the captain was going to fit our ship in anywhere, but I took it for granted he would somehow. So I was surprised to hear the anchor chain unwinding right there in the middle of nothing. I took Patience as my pattern and didn't bat an eye, though. Somebody yelled, "We berth tomorrow. Get your gear then."

How we got ashore was in a rowboat. Being ladies we had to get into it and be cranked down to the water. We got onto the backmost seat of the thing and then down we went. I didn't like it a bit, swinging around fifteen foot up in the air, and without moving my lips I said as much to Patience. She said, "Nobody said being a lady was easier," without moving her lips either. Then a passel of men got in by climbing down a rope net. I'll say my choice would've been the net too.

The captain himself was standing right behind us steering the boat. He gave me a good chance to practice paying no attention to being looked at. I just bore in mind how rich and quirky I was and looked off across the water towards New-York. I couldn't see past the masts but I kept looking, in a careless sort of way.

The captain said, "Excuse me, ma'am," and I remembered about being deaf and didn't move a muscle, but that lady of mine, after all her talk to me! turned around. He said, "If you're strangers to the city, you might like this," and he handed her a little card. "It's a good clean lodging, not too dear, and close to the sights."

Patience said, "Thank you, sir. I'll keep it in mind, if our hosts should weary of us."

Oh, she *was* the right one to do our talking. Who else could think so fast, not to let a boatful of men know we had no place to go and no one meeting us with night coming on? And yet get the exact help we needed? I felt a great worry lift off of me, when that card went safe into her handsack.

It was near dark when we set foot on solid ground but there were lamps standing along the streets and nobody cared about night. What a recklessness about oil they have in that city, to light all outdoors and not even wait till pitch-black to do it, and keep everything going like day-time. I wanted to stand a while and see, but Patience hurried me along. A little brown boy wanted to carry our handbox for pay, but I played I was too rich and quirky to trust him with it. The fronts of the ships stuck in over the street and we walked along under them. I didn't gawk up though.

When we got away from the men from our ship, Patience took out the card. It said Catherine Street. What we were on was South Street. I said we could just go until we found Catherine Street. There couldn't be many streets, even here, I said. But she spoke to the first constable we came to, and he told us where. It wasn't far, but we'd been going just opposite, of course. Once we knew how to go, we got there easy.

And the first one we saw was our captain, climbing the steps of the lodging house. The sight of him stopped us in our tracks, but he said, "Ladies," and bowed.

Patience sailed right up the steps, dignified as could be, head up, saying, "It appears you've found me out,

Captain." I was right behind her, aping her every move but keeping still.

"I have you at a disadvantage, Miss White," he said. "Your brother asked me to help you if I could." Then he unlocked the door and we all went in. He lived there. It was his house. He sent everybody there that he could.

His wife's servants fed the three of us—it was too late for regular supper—and then we passed up the chance to play games in the parlor with the other lodgers. Patience said we were too tired from our journey. I hoped that was a tale.

A servant girl, who was young and pretty and very tired, lit our way up to the third floor. I wanted to at least carry the water pitcher for her, but Patience shook her head when I whispered could I? So many steps we followed that girl up! I was surprised to find my feeling was touched before we got all the way. She was so tired. I wanted to rest her. It could seem that was an unfaithful wish, but I think it just meant my heart was coming to life again.

The girl set the lamp and water down. She said, "Breakfast at half after eight." She left. There was a key in the door. I turned it. I was never in a locked room before. There was a fire going. Nobody could open our door until we let them.

I expected nothing could calm us, on our first chance to stay on and on together and see each other in a room nobody else could open. But we were calm. There was no hurry. I can't say how much it meant that there would never be a hurry again.

I sat back out of the main glow of the lamp watching her lay her things on the dresser and take off her dress and fold it neat and lay it on the other chair. We pretended I wasn't there. It was a game we both knew without having to say, but her cheeks were bright, and she could give me just a glimpse of her back and half her side before her bedgown billowed down and hid her again, and then she undressed the rest of the way inside her bedgown. She washed inside it too, with a soapy cloth she wet in a big white bowl she poured into from the big white pitcher, and she buttoned up to the very top before she washed her teeth. She left the bowl empty and clean. Then she sat cross-legged up on the bed and let her hair fall. I heard the tiny crackling of it lifting by itself to meet her brush. She brushed and brushed. There was no hurry. I saw her neat little toes. I saw her bosom unbound and moving up and down with her arm. Then she made her hair into one big loose braid and slid herself under the bedclothes, and looked at me.

My turn then, to do all the same things, trying to be slow and not look at her, trying to be as beautiful for her as she was for me. She'd have to be the one to tell if I managed to.

I thought, from having sisters, from never being alone to go to bed, I wouldn't be shy like her. I thought I could let her see my whole skin, as easy as a sister, but feeling her eyes on me made me a blushing bride too. I was, to be honest, a little bit vain about my body, and I think I could've forced myself to put down being shy. But I didn't want to force myself, any more than I'd've forced Patience. I wanted us to always do together what felt easiest and naturalest, and when I was down to firpins and band it stopped seeming one bit natural to treat a lovely woman with that look on her face like a sister. So I finished inside my bedgown too, and washed myself inside it. I used her soap, which smelled of lavender, so clean and good.

It brought back all the times I'd held her and loved her and smelled that smell, and I started to long for her so much I almost went to her right then. But I made myself be slow, and wash my mouth with salt and mint, and clean the bowl. Then I took up the lamp and walked over to the bed. I set the lamp on its tall stand there. Outside the wind was smacking the house, a good March window-shaker, cold.

Patience stretched her arm out under the covers and

lifted them, and when I was safe inside she bent arm and covers around me and held me tucked up warm and close like a chick under a wing. Our weight made a hollow in the bed and it bent up around us like a nest. I listened to the wind and thought: I needn't walk in it. I can stay right here with a mother that will never drive me away from her breasts and give them to some new child. All night I can be by her, and drink from her just by tipping my head. I can drink there whenever I can bear to pause from drinking the dear spit of her mouth, and without even leaving her mouth I can take them in my hands, all this heavy softness, and feel the ends pucker into little pebbles, little knots, little fingertips, little buds, little rose hips, pushing into the palms of my hands, all the nights of my life. I can be against her and be warm no matter how sharp the wind may blow, and when I get warm enough I can throw the covers off and let the lamplight show me any part of her I want to see, and she can never be shy with me or hide from me again. Who can count the times the waves will take her unexpected in the deep of a kiss and throw her teeth against my lip and nick it? But she will heal the nick with a touch of her tongue, always, and hug me down to give me the feel of the lovely waves she makes again and again for me, all my nights.

Where are we, high or deep? "Heaven," she says.

We're high then. We stay here so long, like gulls that don't have to move to stay up.

CHAPTER TWO

There was a wink of time next morning when I didn't know where I was or who with, and then I felt Patience breathing beside me, and remembering hit me so sweet I wished I could forget again so I could remember again that same way. But I never forgot again.

I turned my head and looked at her asleep there. What finally made me stop was not getting tired of the sight of her, which could never be, but that I started worrying what time it was, for I'd lost all track.

I stole out of bed careful as a mouse and went and peeked out between the curtains. We had us another bright day, and the sun was just up, which made it six, give or take a quarter. So there was no hurry about getting Patience up. I wanted her to sleep and sleep in her pretty way.

Naturally the fire was long ago gone out, which was nothing I wasn't used to, but my underwear felt like snow to put on because I hadn't thought it would be right to keep it under the covers with me the way I would've back home. Fact is, at the time I didn't think of it. So there I was throwing on my clothes, with my whole body shaking and my teeth snapping together, when I looked over at my darling and she was awake and looking at me and getting ideas. I have to thank that cold underwear for the good sense and self-control I showed. I didn't get a single idea back at her, and it's easy to see how the day would've been spent if I had.

I did take her underwear over and tuck it in beside her to get warm, and she did get her arm around me and try to pull me in, but I said, "Woman, once is enough to get up on a winter's morning."

It did me good to have her want me, and to not be scared to refuse her. There'd been a time when I wouldn't've dast do that, but after last night I could know we felt the same, and I could keep my own opinions and make my own mind up, and be the one to think of all the things we had to get done today.

She said, "You've become sassy overnight," in a way that made me feel she didn't think sassy was very bad.

I said, "If you don't want me sassy, you mustn't do me like you do."

I just never felt so grown-up and worthwhile and proud and able to manage in my whole life before, all because she'd wanted me so much and I'd had enough to give her and make her melt like that and then sleep like that, and wake up with her face full of light.

I said, "You can sleep a little more. It's early yet. I'm going to go look around a little." I knew she wouldn't go back to sleep. It was just a way we both understood, without having to say.

I went downstairs, whistling "I'm Bound for the Kingdom." I couldn't stop myself, but I kept it as low as I could.

The help was all crashing around in the kitchen fixing breakfast. It looked kind of interesting but they didn't have any time for me, so I went and sat in the parlor and looked at a newspaper that was there. It wasn't planned for beginning readers like Garvey was so I had a hard time with it, but it kept me busy and the main thing was it kept me quiet, so when a man lodger came in and my first thought was to ask him, "Are you waiting for *your* wife too?" the newspaper steadied me and I kept my fool mouth shut.

At breakfast the captain told Patience where to go to get passage up the Hudson. He had people in that lodging house from all over, like France and Holland and South Carolina, all of them speaking so outlandish I should've thought they'd play rich and deaf too, but they had plenty of opinions and plenty to say. When they heard where we were going, they just poured out advice and warnings and scarey thoughts until I wished Patience had just kept still. People never can see the good of an idea until it's all done. They didn't scare me, but I worried they might scare Patience. Except I was rich and deaf, I would've asked them what they did other mornings without us for entertainment.

They said our Connecticut banknotes wouldn't be good out in Genesee. They said speculators had grabbed up all the best farms and ordinary folk couldn't hope for anything but scrub. They said the British might come swooping down out of Canada any time, like they did before when they burned Buffalo. The British didn't want us filling up the West and getting to be a great nation, they said. "Jealous," one said. "No, terrified," another one said, which didn't make entirely pleasant listening either but at least it took their minds off of us.

There were women lodging there too, as their regular home. I had it from Patience that there'd been women like us before, because the Bible complained of them, so I naturally wondered right away about these two, but they claimed to be mother and daughter, and after I looked at them a little better I got to believe it, and anyway their faces didn't shine. I almost sighed out loud. I so much wanted somebody to tell.

Patience wrote a note to Parson and signed my name to it, even though I told her he'd know better than to think

I could handle a quill so perfect and elegant in this short
while, or ever. She wrote that my friend Miss Patience
White and I were in the city briefly and would like leave to
call at the convenience of the Reverend Mr. Peel and Mrs.
Peel. Patience hired one of the captain's servants to carry
the note to Parson's house, and before it seemed possible
the servant was back.

I thought he probably hadn't even gone at all, but no,
he had a note from Mrs. Peel saying she'd been longing to
know me and she couldn't be more delighted, and she'd
be pleased to fetch us as soon after noon as was reasonable, say one o'clock.

It was heartwarming to get such a note, and an all-
round relief, but I got such a strange little nervous feeling
like I was accountable for Mrs. Peel and maybe Patience
would think she didn't amount to much, being so friendly
and folksy and not like a New Englander. And maybe
Patience would think Parson was an ordinary man, or
light or silly or weak or foppish.

Patience read the note over again. She said, "I believe
she wrote this standing up and in a hurry." I stayed
nervous. Patience said, "I wonder if everyone in New-
York is so warm and open-hearted?" I started hoping.
She said, "Oh, sweetheart! Maybe we're out of stingy
country at last!" So I smiled and smiled, until I com-
menced to wonder what Parson and his wife would think
of Patience. Must be I just liked to worry.

Being crammed into the end of an island like that meant
the houses had to be hooked together and couldn't have
yards and had to be too tall and have too many stairs, but
it also meant New-York was a handy town to get around
in, not much ground to cover. Patience went by a little
map the captain drew for us, and we found the Albany
Basin without trouble even though it was on the other side
of town. I thought she was so brilliant, telling how to turn

all those corners by a map, but then she showed me how and it was easy.

The basin had a couple of steamboats in it. Patience thought we ought to study them and see if knowing something would take some of my scare out, but it was clear to me that knowing more just meant getting scareder. I wouldn't go look and she stayed by me. She wasn't scared. She has a liking for the new. But bad enough we had to ride on one of those boats, without looking at it first and brooding, I figured. I just wished we couldn't hear either, that sound like a million tuckered-out horses, like a wild teakettle the size of a house. But it could do in a day what sail took two weeks at, and cost less to boot, so what to do? I sort of knew it wouldn't really hurt us. I was just scared of having a scared feeling.

The agent said the cheap Albany boat was making up a cargo and would leave when it was made. We should have our trunks brought over and ask back every day, he said, and meanwhile enjoy New-York. It was such a comfort to be with Patience and not feel obliged to scowl. He smiled and she smiled, so I allowed myself a little smile too, and when we walked away, she said, "It must be our happy faces. There's a saying, which I now see the truth of, that all the world loves a lover."

It was really very bad of her to take my breath away in the middle of a street full of drays and dray horses like that. She just smiled at my problem, and try as I might I couldn't feel very cross.

After dinner I couldn't keep myself away from the parlor window, but Patience kept calm and read. It seemed a good long wait for Mrs. Peel, but that was just me. I won't speak against that good warm woman. She was *not* late, she did *not* keep us waiting, and finally there she was. I knew her by Potiphar. He looked so odd, a big strong horse like him pulling a little light city rig, but he was still my dear Potiphar and the sight of him pleased me so.

I rushed right out without my cloak to give him a hug. He was a kindhearted horse and he took my hug even if he didn't remember me. How could he know me when I had on a dress and smelled of lavender and Patience? When I said, "Potiphar! Potiphar, honey horse!" he moved his ears like something stirred in his memory. At least my voice was the same.

Then I got up my nerve and looked back at the rig where Mrs. Peel was. She was a sort of plumpish, sort of plain-faced woman, giving me a friendly looking-over. "It's Sam, at last," she said. "I'm sorry to be late."

I said no, no, she wasn't late, and then Patience came down the steps and put my cloak around me and nodded at Mrs. Peel with just a touch of New England frost about her. I was afraid she was blaming Mrs. Peel that I ran out in the cold to hug a horse, but I later found out Patience was shy. I'd've never guessed it, her with nothing to be shy about.

Mrs. Peel said, "Miss White—Sam—do get in," and right while we were still climbing up she set to talking in a way some folks might've thought meant she wanted to be noticed, but I knew it was so we'd feel easy. Just knowing she wanted us to did the job for me. She said how Parson'd told her all about me (which I kind of doubted), and how she'd been so envious because he was the one who got to know me while she stayed home and gave pianoforte lessons to empty-headed, soft, silly, *ordinary* girls.

She said, "I told him another summer I'd go with him. I would *not* let him be the only one to have adventures. Or I'd get a van and start off for myself. Disguised as Dan Peel, of course." And she laughed, like she knew plain enough she could never look slender and elegant, and like she didn't fret about it. She said, "And I'd keep my eyes open for a boy to help me. I'd do it, too, except that I'm afraid my boy would turn out to be really a boy."

It was a relief to see Patience's face turn friendly. I was afraid she might think Mrs. Peel was a touch hearty, a touch common, but Patience knew the same as me how uncommon that much kindness is.

In just a few squares—hardly worth hitching up Potiphar for except to show good will—we came to Little George Street and the Peel house and had us a fine welcome on the front steps from Parson and a whole crew of little Peel boys and girls who'd heard all about me too. And I knew that my own natural way was what was wanted, and that it would be an awful disappointment all around if I was to act like a lady. I just hoped Patience knew so too.

Parson said, "You've gone and changed. You'll have a fight making me believe you're still Sam at heart," and he smiled back and forth between Patience and me in a little quiet happy way that made me think he saw everything about us and thought it was grand.

I said, "Patience is fixing me, but it's uphill work."

The children begged, "Don't fix her, don't fix her!" If only for that I would've liked them.

I liked the whole family of them, and I just wished they had a better house, worthy of them. It wasn't bad from the outside, tall and narrow, about what a house had to be in New-York. But inside it was all outdoors brought in, all the messes that belong to be outside, like animals and plants and even a bird, and you could work night and day without getting ahead of a house like that, or making it the kind of fresh neat place Parson's van was. And naturally a woman like Mrs. Peel, with her mind on other things, didn't work night and day or have much chance of making her hired help do it. You could see why Parson had to get away summers.

Everything cloth was in shreds, and everything wood was scratched deep. Nobody's got mice enough to need that many cats. There was a soft gray layer of cat hair on everything, including on us after we'd been there a while. Be softheaded about kittens and see what comes of it. I'm not being picky. I always let Pa be the one to drown kittens myself. But I think if I'd lived in Parson's house I could've brought myself to it.

There was a dog too, if such an odd pale flat-faced critter is entitled to the name. But it yapped like a dog, more or less, and had doggy feet so I guess that settles it. Mrs. Peel was fond of it and let it get up on her lap, which shows again how big her heart was. It had a little curled-over tail like a hog. It was a lot like a hog, except the feet.

The bird was called a parrot. The children were very proud of it. They made us look at it first thing, and I will say it was a sight, like painted. It was in a cage made of bendy wood. The children said it was unhappy there and it should be on a stand but the cats would get it then. I said, "I'd lay my money on the bird," and I would too. It was built on the plan of an eagle. It could've been a help with the cats. They claimed it could talk, but it never did in my hearing. They claimed it was talking Dutch. That may or may not be so. I knew *they* believed it, but with somebody like Parson around you have to add a pinch of salt, and they didn't know that yet. They begged and begged it to say, "Pretty Polly," and finally it let out a squawk that with a lot of fancy could be taken for that, about like sometimes at night you can fancy the wind is saying something. But to humor them we said yes, sure enough, it truly says Pretty Polly.

They put on a regular show for us, playing the piano-forte, and speaking pieces they had by heart, and showing us pictures they'd made, and examples of their handwriting, and how they could read and turn somersets, until Parson got tired of it all and sent them upstairs.

Ordinarily I wouldn't like to see children put themselves forward like that, but I could see they only did it to give us the best things they had. The biggest one could read better than me. I was about like the second one.

Then there was a chance to talk to Parson. Patience and Mrs. Peel were jawing and laughing on the other side of the Parlor. I think they were comparing Parson and me like any two regular husbands. At least I overheard Patience say, "Mine never had enough cake. I intend to see that she gets all she wants."

I sure liked hearing her call me "mine," even if it did make me blush and Parson smile. There was no hiding anything from him, not that I cared to hide. The problem was to keep from bragging. I wanted to listen some more, but Parson began asking about our trip and our plans.

While I was telling him the children came stealing down the stairs, and when Parson didn't yell them back up again, they took encouragement and came on in and sat on my lap and beside me and at my feet. They didn't bother us. We kept on talking.

Parson said that prices were going up very fast in the Purchase, which was his name for Genesee, because there was going to be a canal run right through it and open it all up. He said the State Assembly was absolutely certain to pass the bill this spring, and just the thought of it had shot up land prices all along the line.

"It's bad for the kind of price you hoped for," he said, "and it's bad for the turnpike towns along the Hudson, but it's a wonderful thing. Think of it! A ditch three hundred and fifty miles long, floating barges full of wheat and corn and lumber from the Great Lakes to the Hudson!"

I said, "Well, that'll be some ditch, uphill and down. Water might be a little deeper in the valleys than on the hilltops."

He explained about locks.

I could see how it might be done, and the heart went out of me. Then I saw the real flaw of it all. "What's to keep the ditch water from running down the first river it crosses?" I asked him.

He explained about aqueducts. A bridge to get a boat across a river! Any fool could see they'd never manage that, but why did they have to think they could and ruin land prices the very year Patience and me wanted to buy a farm?

Parson said, "So buy. In twenty years you'll sell your farm for city lots, and be rich."

"Sell our *farm?* Who could be that? Anyhow, I don't want to be rich. I just want to live with my—I want to live with Patience and be happy."

"You just want to live," he said, not as a question.

"With Patience," I said.

"My understanding was that you wanted to bring the wilderness to its knees and call yourself king of all you looked upon."

"If Patience wants that. I want something more like what we can hope to do."

"Last summer it was what you wanted."

"I've had to get sensible since then. With somebody to take care of now. If one is foolish, the other must be sensible. If Patience was sensible, I'd still be foolish."

Patience must've heard me say her name because she got up and sat in a nearer chair, and Mrs. Peel dragged over the stool from the pianoforte. They sat there waiting for what we'd say next. We couldn't think of anything we wanted them to hear.

But the little girl on my lap had plenty to say. She was about eight. She had big new teeth half grown in, and rosy cheeks, and shiny brown hair. Her name was Dora. She'd been patting my cheek and chin and throat for quite a while, and now she said, "I would always have known you weren't a boy." She talked very fast, to make use of us keeping still. She said, "You know what my favorite Sam story is? It's how one morning Papa couldn't find his shaving kit, and he looked and looked and *looked* for it."

Parson was looking at me with a look that was half prayer and half laugh, and holding his breath.

Dora said, "And he asked you if you had it, and you didn't, and if you knew where it went, and you didn't, and he had to ask if he could borrow *yours*."

The other children couldn't keep still past that point, so they all yelled out the rest: "And you didn't *have* one. And you had to admit, you're a *girl!*"

I bent my head back and laughed until I noticed Patience looking extra-ladylike to make up for me, and then I stopped and said, yes, that was my favorite story too. I said, "Every time I think on it, I laugh like I never heard it before."

With her little hand on my face again, Dora said, "But that was silly of Papa. I would have always known."

I said, "Well, he didn't have your advantages."

I was glad to be able to make Parson look as happy as he did then, except he maybe carried it too far. He maybe made it run over into relief, like he never did find out till then that I can say the right thing sometimes.

He was just so pleased with me that he invited us to go to a show with him and Mrs. Peel that evening. "Nothing fancy—we'll sit in the pit," he said. "It's something you should see while you're here. *Nights in Naughty New-York.*"

I thought to say I had something else naughty planned, but I wasn't sure I wanted to call it naughty, and while I was thinking up another way to say no, I looked at Patience and she was smiling and her eyes were shining and I could see she wanted to go something fierce.

It gave me a little turn to see she wasn't in the same hurry as me to get back to Heaven. And another little turn to see I couldn't, from now on, just say yes or no without finding out what she wanted too. It was kind of a hard lesson to get ahold of. I won't say I learned it once and for all right then. But I did get a start on it.

I said, "We'd be pleased," and then while they all made

plans I thought about how if Patience could make me wait and wish, I could do the same to her, and if what she wanted counted, so did what I wanted, and another time, I thought, I'll weight my own wish as heavy as hers before I say yes. And I thought, here I am worried sick about land prices and where to find a place for us, and here she is wanting to see a silly show. Of course she didn't *know* about the canal and all there was to worry about, and what a strain it was to play the man's part and think about dull hard things like land prices. I wanted to spare her, but I did wish I could tell her just enough to make her grateful that I bore it all alone.

After supper at our lodging, we met Parson and his wife and walked to the theater. There was no use taking Potiphar, Parson said—no place to leave him.

I was all settled into a fret, and half enjoying it. I couldn't help thinking I made a pretty good man. There was Patience, so light and silly, laughing with Mrs. Peel, and there I was, as gloomy as Pa, trudging along beside Parson, asking him where *he* thought we should go.

"For cheap land close to market?" he asked.

"Yes."

"My Susquehanna Turnpike bonds have dropped enough to make me guess the bottom's fallen out of Greene County. If all you want to do is live, in a country that's cleared and settled and safe, you could do it there."

"Is it far?"

"No, it's near. About ninety miles. It's on the Hudson. You'll pass it. It's the first county this side of Albany County. It's freehold. The patroons missed it."

"Maybe they didn't want it," I said.

"Maybe."

"Reckon it should be looked at. No sense getting way out west and then wondering."

"No. You could do worse than look at it."

"Don't mention it to Patience?"

Parson grinned and said, "I won't, Sam. I can hold my tongue as well as you. Thank you for that."

We got to the theater. It was all bright paint and bright lamps and noise and stink. At least down in the pit it was stink. I won't say any one city man stunk worse than any one farmer, but you don't generally find farmers bunched up like that, and smoking cigars, and spitting. I looked at Patience, to get her to make some sign she'd liefer be alone in bed with me. She made a little face and wrinkled her nose, to show she wasn't overfond of every single thing here, but it was plain to see she was happy and excited and while she had an ounce of fight left in her she wouldn't leave. I was near sick, but she most needed a millstone in her lap to keep from flying right off the bench. I just had to shake my head.

Then some horns and fiddles started and the big curtains opened up, and some girls and men came prancing out, all decked out so bright, singing and jangling things in their hands and whirling around and smiling, and I swear, I felt like a fool to feel it, but I never felt so cheerful in my life. I just didn't have the grip I thought I did on being manlike.

The crowd let out a yell and clap, me right along, and everybody was so ready to laugh it didn't matter what was said. I'm still studying on some of the jokes. Like, this farmer boy that was one of the heroes? I mean, these two farmer boys come to the city—kind of like Patience and me, I see. And this one farmer boy says, "How fur north must I walk, to get to the North River?" That's one of the jokes I study on yet, but at the time I laughed right along, till the tears came, and Patience too.

(One mistake people make is thinking actors sink to going onto the stage, like any other form of going bad. I want to say, I believe they do it because they get an ambition to, men and women both. They want to do what will bring that love and happiness up at them, I believe.)

Afterwards, Mrs. Peel, who had a gift that way, remembered quite a few of the songs and hummed them as we walked along the street.

It all made a little speck of cheerfulness in a nervous time, and later the memory came and livened many a dull day. But it couldn't brighten the whole of its own night. I had a new worry that came at me when we got alone again.

My mind was clear on where to go—Greene County, no matter what it was like—but the worry was getting Patience to agree to it. Her with her dreams of being heroes and homesteaders and shoulder-to-shoulder and all.

Well, I'd told her plain I wouldn't take her to wild country or let her think I would. But did she remember that? And if she did, did she think she'd change it all somehow? And if I was foolish enough to talk it over with her, was there any hope she'd be sensible?

I just wished I knew a sure-fire way to have my own way. Did Pa ask Ma what she thought about going to the Hooestennuc Valley? She went and she made-do, that's all. At the time it riled me for Ma's sake, but that night in New-York I saw there was a lot to be said for a way where there's no backtalk and everybody's place is set.

We went up the two sets of stairs to our room, me first and Patience behind me, tickling me through my skirt and laughing and whispering what we'd do when our door was shut again, and I swear I was near as cross at her as if I'd already spoke of Greene County and heard her say unreasonable things about the frontier.

I almost didn't even love her, because I couldn't say, "That's it, woman! Now get used to it!" It just felt beneath me, somehow, to be sneaky and sly and plotting how to get her to stop at Greene County without letting on why. I blamed it all on her. If only she'd had good sense, I could be my regular aboveboard self. Didn't it show how open I generally was, that Parson was relieved I could tell a lie?

Patience turned the key and pitched her bonnet away. She was already too hot to stand it in the cold room, and she said, "Get down here, you tall child, where I can kiss you," and she opened my clothes and touched me all the places she'd taught me to like best, except then I didn't like it, for feeling guilty at what I meant to do. But I played glad, and kissed her too, to keep her wild for me so I could get my own way. And she was burrowing at me, saying, "Where's my wet? Where's my melt?" and I didn't have them to give her.

I said, "My chest ached all day from what I gave you last night," which was true, and she bent her head at the thought and was satisfied, I think—she had a little tiny cocky smile.

Oh, how could I treat her so? It can be said for Pa, at least, that he didn't work on Ma's feeling for him, to get his way. But maybe he would've, if she'd had some.

Next morning we dressed, not shy, and then she sat on my lap while we waited for the call to breakfast. She was full of kisses, which I tipped my chin up for, and she was full of plans for how to get the most out of our last day in the city. She said, "I want to see the ships come up the bay, and all the flags, and I want to buy some paints and brushes. The *colors,* darling! You can't think what I saw advertised in the newspaper. Purple lake and Federal drab and Hartford smoke. I may not dare buy, but I have to see, don't you think? And garnet and crow."

"Patience?" I said, quite weak and soft—guilty.

"And dragon's blood. And olive."

I figured before breakfast was my last chance that day to make use of the special weakness for me she got by being on my lap, so I kept saying, "Patience? Patience?" till she started hearing.

She said, "What is it, sweetheart?"

"Did I tell you about my uncle?"

"Someday you really must tell me all about all of your uncles."

"That lives in Greene County? A brother of Ma's?"

"*Does* he?"

"Maybe we'll never come back—"

"Who knows?"

"—we won't. And I want to see him, and my cousins, and all, fore we get too far and never come back."

She was putting her mouth here and there on my head and huffing warm down through my hair to my scalp. "Back from where?" she whispered.

"Oh, Michigania, or Ohio, or wherever we go."

"Don't be silly. We're going to Genesee," she said, huffing on my neck then, not suspicious.

"Or even Genesee. We won't even come back from Genesee. And there's my uncle I never got to see. And my cousins."

"I guess we could. Where did you say they are?"

"Greene County. Right on our way. We'll pass it tomorrow on the river. I want to stop."

"You want to?" she asked. I knew I had her. "All right, darling."

Oh, I just get sick remembering.

And that day I couldn't eat my breakfast. I hoped Patience thought I was too excited. She ate hers all right and talked to the other lodgers. I was glad to be rich and deaf.

Looking back I can see that the day was interesting, and everyone was kind to us. At the bank where Patience changed her Connecticut banknotes for York State ones, there was a fine old banker who looked us over and liked us and got to talking with Patience. She wouldn't've wanted me to talk to strange men like that, but she did lots of things she wouldn't've wanted me to do. He asked where we were bound, the very question she'd warned me not to answer, and she told him Genesee with a stop first in Greene County, and he said, "Poor old Greene County. Land's going there for a song. You can get a good farm now for eight hundred dollars. Forty good acres for that! What a pity!" I guess if you think it's a pity depends on if you're a banker or a farmer, and if you're buying or selling. I just wanted to pull her away. It wasn't till later I came to see how that banker was a fine old man, and that he likely saw about us, and wished us luck.

It was a day to remember all right. We went to a Mechanical Panorama, and a *flea* circus which was a cheat because the fleas didn't do all the things the sign said they would, like dance and play ball, but just walked around like any other fleas except they had little balls and things tied to them. We went to the Museum of Natural Curiosities, and it was a cheat too, saying it had a two-headed calf and you could easy see the wires holding the other head on. Still there'd've been a way to enjoy even the cheats, if it hadn't been so heavy on my heart about my lie.

And dear Patience was doing everything to please me, asking didn't I want some cherry soda water? a hot muffin? an orange? They had vendors all over. I tried an orange, not to keep saying no, but I felt so foul I couldn't stomach it. In the end I slipped it to a hog when Patience wasn't looking.

After supper we walked out again. Would I like to hear a philosophical lecture? Look at the stars through a telescope? I near said no, but caught myself. If she wanted to, it was the least I could do. Let *her* enjoy herself, anyhow, I thought. The philosophical lecture was about how people and animals and plants are made of billions of little boxes stuck together, too little to see. I wonder about that.

In bed I played dead-tired and stayed apart from her, and played asleep until I felt her sleep, which wasn't soon, and then I rolled on my back and stared at the coals of our fire dying away, and when there was barely anything left to them I got up and lit a spill and carried it to the lamp.

When I got the lamp going, I looked down at Patience and thought how I mustn't break her rest and how there was nothing to say that couldn't wait, and right during such thoughts I bent and petted her hair and kissed her and said, "Patience, wake up. Wake up, Patience. I got something to tell."

She sat right up, scared, saying, "What?"

And even knowing I was fixing it so she'd never believe another word I said, or trust me in anything, and maybe not even love me, which would mean I couldn't stand to stay alive, I said, "That was a tale, about my uncle and them. And we needn't stop at Greene County. We'll make out somehow, wherever you want to go, if you'll still have me."

She sat there blinking and scowling and shaking her head, like to get a bug out of her ear, and I had to tell it all three or four times over before she got it straight, her being just awake and not ever thinking I might be a liar. I can't say it got easier to tell. My tongue kept sticking to the top of my mouth, but I kept on till she had it all clear and then she said, puzzled, "Why? Why?" so I told why, which was even worse, and then I just stood there feeling so brained and gutted I couldn't even be scared. I knew I'd lost my chance in life and I knew I'd deserved to.

My eyes blurred over, which was all to the good because I didn't want to see her face when it wasn't full of love for me, and finally I just let myself drop down crosswise of the bed, outside of the covers, face down. She kept so quiet.

I thought how she'd trusted herself to me and promised her brother to never go back. I felt so sorry for her—a little softish lady, plumpish, not overyoung, kind of weak, no part of her tough. I thought to ask her to let me stay with her till she got settled somewhere. Maybe she could keep school right here in the city. I thought to say, where

Parson and Mrs. Parson could help her get new friends and maybe she could love somebody who'd be better and finer than me, more her own kind, man or woman, and the thought made me bite the quilt and groan like the thought of just dying never could. Her mouth, her bosom, her breath, her warm wet, her melt, for someone else! I lifted up from the quilt and let my groans be loud. Let her think I was playing for pity—I was. Let her worry I'd be heard. Maybe she'd hold me and still me if she worried enough.

So she came by me and held me, saying, "Don't, Sarah. Hush."

I couldn't talk, but I could whisper. "You've got to see how sorry I am and let me off."

"Nothing is so terrible."

"Oh, *real* terrible. But love me anyhow?"

"I have to. What else can I do?"

I knew what else she could do, and groaned again. "Say you don't fault me."

"Fault you? No, lamb."

I couldn't stop being puffy right away, but I could smile.

She said, "I think a lie you can't go to sleep without confessing is no great harm."

"Don't say it's no harm, because it is. Just say you can still love me."

I raised my head then and opened my eyes so I could see if to believe her in case she said it, and I saw something I needed more than love right then. I saw she wanted me, and I knew she couldn't unless the rest was settled. And it didn't matter that somewhere in the back of my mind I was still worried where we'd end up and how I'd take care of her. With my heart cleared of its lie, I could want her again too.

I rolled over to my back, to make whatever she might want easy for her, and looked at her face, and stayed very still and quiet.

BOOK FIVE

Patience

CHAPTER ONE

I said "Of course I do, of course I love my Sarah," which was true, always, but then I said, "Of course I'm not angry," and that was not, though I thought it was until I began touching her with hand and lip and noticed in myself a temptation to be not quite gentle.

I was so shocked at myself I had to draw away from her. I thought, but I am tender, I am only tender, always and only tender.

She stayed as she was, not even turning her head to look at me.

"You *are* angry," she whispered.

"No. But I want—"

She waited without moving.

It took me a minute or more to admit the rest: "To bite you."

"It's all right."

"No! How could I want to hurt you?"

"Because I tricked you."

"That only makes us even. Didn't I trick you into living with me? Couldn't I have kept Martha out just by locking the door, and let us go on and on the way you wanted to? I'm glad to be evened up."

"You don't act like you're glad," Sarah said. "Come by me like before. Don't be clear over there."

"Don't tell me what to do!" I said. Her bedgown was old

and soft, easy to rip. "You didn't like the day I gave you! I wanted to delight you and you wouldn't be delighted! You made me afraid a whole long day that you'd stopped loving me! You gave the orange I bought you to a hog! Lie to me if you must, but don't you ever again refuse to be delighted when I am giving you something!" And I caught her side in my teeth and clung there, hard. She stayed still and unresisting and stretched out like a sacrifice and let me learn what besides tenderness my love was made of, until my anger was completely gone and all our sweetness came flowing easily back.

Much later, when we had satisfied almost everything but sleepiness, I said, "Dear little girl, I hope I didn't hurt you too much." (A lie.)

"You didn't," she said peacefully. (A lie too, I thought.)

But next morning when we looked for a mark there was none. And I'd clamped my teeth so hard! I wonder if it is generally true that a heightened woman can't be marked.

And is it generally true, I wonder, that being united in love refreshes better than sleep? (Oh, I wish Sarah and I had someone we could talk about these things with.)

We woke refreshed, after what could not have been more than minutes of sleep. I wanted nothing so much as to mend Sarah's bedgown, but it was the morning for taking our boat up the Hudson River, and I had to forgo the delicious false penitence and secret pride of that task. The boat wouldn't wait, so the bedgown must.

Our daily inquiries after the progress of the loading had made the steamboat agent know and like us. "This is the day, ladies," he said. "A passage for two to Albany, right?"

"To Greene County, please," I said.

Sarah said, "Patience! You needn't!" She took my arm and shook it. "I explained. You needn't. I'll go wherever you want."

The agent got a little treat from watching that. He looked back and forth between us with great interest and perfect good will, as well as some doubt as to our destination. I settled his mind by pushing the money through the wicket. "To Greene County," I said.

"That's to the city of Hudson," he said. "You'll have to get you a ferry across the river there. The dock at Kaatskill's still abuilding. You got kin there? You ever been there before? You figure to settle there?"

"Miss Dowling has an uncle there," I said, to have a little laugh at Sarah.

He said, "Well, get on board anytime. She'll sail when she's got the tide to boost her along. If anything happens, hold your breath. Don't breathe the steam is all."

So we climbed the gangplank. Sarah was afraid, her eyes big like a child's, but she kept up with me. The boilers were building pressure, getting ready, making a noise like nothing I'd ever heard. Like a dragon, perhaps. A herd of dragons. The deck pulsed under our feet like a panting dog, and it was hot though the wind off the harbor was cold.

"I've heard these things do blow up," Sarah said.

"And carriages overturn, and horses throw their riders, and walkers fall into pits, and oxen gore, and if we tried I'm sure we could smother in our beds." ("Bed," I amended in a whisper.) "Trees fall, lightning strikes. Let her blow!" (I whispered, "I don't care, while we're together.")

"Maybe you better hold my hand, so we won't get blowed apart," she whispered.

I took her hand. It was natural to feel timid and hold together. All the ladies were doing it. If I hadn't taken her hand someone else would have. She looked so darling, tall and worried there.

And late in the morning the tide came up the bay and up the river and our pilot nudged us out into it and the people on the deck waved and called, "Goodbye, good-

bye," to the people on the dock who were shouting something our engines drowned out, but I read their lips and
it was "goodbye" too. The way west was first north, up the
Hudson. Not many of us would ever come back.

Midstream, the boat set to in earnest, so *fast*. A horse
can gallop that fast, or seem to. It can make the wind
whistle past your ears that way, for a little while. But a
horse gets tired, and our wonderful big paddle wheels
never did, and the tide behind us gave us the whole
weight of the sea as a shove. I held Sarah's hand and felt
the ancient sea and the new wheels carry us to a life we
had no pattern for, that no one we knew of had ever
lived, that we must invent for ourselves on a razor's edge,
and I tipped my head back and sang three hallelujahs.

Sarah, in a little time, grew accustomed, like anyone
else who farms a volcano, but I held her hand until the
other ladies calmed down too and ceased to cling together.

It was not possible to talk, so much surrounded. I could
not think of a single thing to say that was fit for a lady
to overhear, and Sarah was still under my command to be
silent.

It was a strange day, silently riding that tall rushing
house between the miles of cliffs and mountains and vil-
lages, eagles and mansions and waving children. I thought
it would come back in my dreams. It was so much like
a dream already. I found my head full of vast meaningless
truths, such as life is a river, which I am grateful not to
have had an opportunity to express. That's the kind of day
it was, unreal, and at sunset the hills to the right—the
Berkshire Hills—caught the yellow light and were very
beautiful. Night came fully dark, but we kept on, steering
perhaps by farmhouse windows, and at a little after
eight Sarah and I and our three trunks and our one handbox were deposited at the steamboat landing of the city
of Hudson, New York State.

We took a room in Hudson and slept as though we'd
walked those miles, and in the morning a ferryboat rowed

by many slaves took us across and down to Kaatskill. We left the trunks and all at the ferry landing and walked around.

Kaatskill was so busy then, full of drovers and wagons, a turnpike town with goods to store and travelers to feed. I couldn't believe it was dying, but Sarah had Parson Peel's word for it, and the banker had said the same, and in eight more years, yes, the turnstiles stopped turning and the pikes grew grass.

To buy land you *know* will drop in value! But the big-mouths at the boarding house in New-York had scared my Sarah, and Parson Peel had scared her, and we'd come to a stopping place, and what *did* we want, as Sarah said, but to live? Didn't Columbus himself aim for India and find America as something as a letdown?

"Shall we stay?" I asked.

"I believe we ought," she said.

It was March 27, 1817.

We took a pleasant room in a Kaatskill lodging house, and then began the process of finding a farm, a matter neither simple nor swift.

Even letting our intention be known was not simple because it was not feminine. I did not know how. As Edward had said, men make the world go. How does a woman go up to a strange man and announce that she wants to buy a bit of it? Can a woman approach the court-house loiterers or the tavern or the docks and ask for news of real estate? The problem was peculiarly vexing because we had not anticipated it. There would be a public list, there would be a land office, there would be notices in the newspaper. There would be anything except this staring dry-mouthed at each other and wondering how to begin.

Sarah even offered to cut her hair again and be our man, if a man was so much needed, and the thought rallied my womanly pride enough to make it possible, after all, to speak to the banker when I deposited our money, and to the drayman who brought our trunks up from the landing, and to the postmaster when I posted a letter to tell Edward where we were. And the storekeeper, and the farmer's boy who brought eggs to our landlady, and the stablekeeper where I asked after livery rates, and in a day or two the word was around that two eccentric Yankee females with more money than sense were in the market for a farm. We liked that description of ourselves so well that we decided it was time to let Sarah speak again.

We began to hear about farms. So many farmers wanted to move on. Only we wanted a farm in Greene County. Soon I could no longer remember just why we did. Sarah claimed that she still knew why.

Each farm had to be gone to, by hired horse and buggy, looked at, walked around on, thought about, judged, compared with the others. We told each other we would not be hasty in a choice that meant comfort or ruin for the rest of our days. We needn't stay in Greene County at all, we said, unless it really pleased us. Even as we said that, we must have known we had to stay. We'd spent too much for lodging and hiring a horse to start the same long business again somewhere else.

But how judge a winter field? How weigh what a farmer who wants to sell out may assert about the yield per acre? How prefer one slaty hillside to another? I was not a good companion night or day. I was too nervous. Sarah claimed she wasn't nervous. It was not hard to tell a good farm from a bad one in any season, she claimed. Something about the kinds of trees and the growth they'd made. Something about the kind of ball the soil made in her hand. I didn't question her very hard. One of us had to know, and it could not be I. If she didn't, I didn't want to be told so.

All I knew was the price we should pay, because the banker in New-York had told us; we could go to eight hundred for forty acres, but it must be soon while there was that much left.

At the end of April, we were still looking. That is, Sarah was. To cut the livery charges we'd given up the buggy. Sarah rode out alone on horseback. I stayed at our lodging and sewed for her. I was glad not to go, not to be party to the endless solemn tedious country dickering, so full of pauses, so reluctant to name a figure. Sarah enjoyed it. Let her do it, I thought.

But some evenings she didn't get back to Kaatskill until after dark and I could not endure many of those. By day I could sew almost peacefully, but come dark I had to have her by me. At first she couldn't even see why. Didn't I trust her?

The lodging was no place to discuss it, so we walked down to the Hudson and sat, a little apart, on the fresh spring grass. It was a moonlit night.

Sarah said, "When I do get back, you hardly ever love me. So what does it matter?"

"I worry when you're out after dark."

"You didn't worry back home. You *made* me be out, back home."

"That was different," I said.

"To me it seems no different, except now I'm on a horse and then I was afoot."

"It's different," I repeated, to keep my position simple and unassailable.

She said, "I'm looking for a place for us. Should I look just nearby and miss the faraway that might be better, to hurry back to you, when you won't love me?"

"Stop saying that. You know I love you."

"Oh, Patience, I get scared. Like what if you just want to be friends after all, and what if you don't need what I do? I get so scared."

"I love you. I need what you need." I took her hand.

"Then you should kiss me. You should hold me."

"You get excited. I don't dare."

"Well, sure I do. But we got something to do for that. When did you start figuring it was a bad thing?"

"Not bad. Unwise. When you started being noisy, darling."

"Am I?"

"Don't you hear yourself?"

"Just some hard breathing. Maybe a sigh."

"You groan like a woman in childbed, sweetheart. I don't want people to think I'm beating you. I've been saying you have nightmares."

"Who *to?*" she asked, much offended.

"To the ladies. The lodgers. First time they asked, 'Why, what was that noise in your room last night?' Since then they've said, 'Oh, poor Miss Dowling had another dream last night and you took so long to wake her from it I near came in myself.' I think we should be sparing, don't you?"

Sarah said, embarrassed, "All right. But you might've told me before stead of letting me get so scared." She was silent and then she laughed. She said, "I feel foolish about it, and yet somehow—vain too. I can be sparing, now I know you still want me. I can wait."

"Well, hurry with our place. Because I can't wait." I kissed her hand and pressed it to my bosom. I said, "When we have our place, I think you'll find me ardent enough. We haven't begun to use our ardor. I long to give you all of mine."

"You'd better kiss me before we go back."

"I'd better not," I said.

We walked back along the main street, past the taverns and inns loud with rivermen and drovers and teamsters. I remembered how once I had envied men because they could have what I needed but could not have. But they couldn't, after all, have what I needed.

After all my explanation, in bed Sarah wanted to kiss me. I wouldn't let my toes tingle for her and she got discouraged and stopped. She whispered, "I'm putty in your hands, but you can always say no to me. Why is that?"

"Because I'm older than you. Be back every day by dark, and find us our place, and someday you may be older than I."

The state of Sarah's wardrobe made another urgency. She had worn the same dress every day since we left Connecticut, and though her own sweet body could never soil it, the smell of horse began to be powerful before I had her new dress finished. The new one was made of the same almond wool as the other. My thought was to make it seem she had a dozen dresses, all the same. Not just from pride, though pride was part of it, but as a protection; I was willing for us to seem eccentric or subject to an occasional nightmare, but never piteous or helpless or poor.

Those could have been somewhat pleasant days, if I hadn't been so generally nervous. I sat in the parlor with the other ladies, merchants' wives whose husbands were inland, up the turnpike, on business. It was eccentric too, of course, to be making something so large and useful as a dress while the ladies worked at needlepoint and satin stitch, but they did not too severely frown on me. Loving Sarah had freed all my tender feelings for women. I could always find in my heart an excuse for anything any woman did, and how could they earnestly disapprove of anyone who felt that way?

They put in many an hour of mystified speculation about Sarah and me, while I stitched away and was pleasant and evasive. Where did we come from? "The East," I said. But where in the East? "Just—East," I said. They devised, a bit at a time, beautiful tales of blighted love for both of us, which I looked mysteriously pensive over. Two heartsore maidens seeking solace from mutual misfortune through mutual sympathy, and fleeing the scene of their despair, a place so painful that even its name could not be uttered. Somewhere in that tear-drenched country, the men we loved lay—buried? Or strolled unfeelingly with the wives we could only hate and envy? I couldn't choose my favorite speculation, and by my silence let them all seem possible.

The ladies found me odd but lovable, and I admired their needlework. However it came out, the aim was beauty. To show that I aimed for beauty sometimes too, I showed them my paintings which I got out of the trunk the day I put the scraps of almond wool back into it. And since she really liked it and could afford it, and since I didn't much like it anymore, I let the fiercest lady—the most unhappy one—buy "Moses Destroying the Golden Calf." She needed it and I didn't; I didn't feel fierce anymore.

She offered me a dollar for it. That was the first money I ever made as a painter, and I'm glad it was from a merchant's wife. To merchants and their families the giving and taking of money seems quite natural, not at all awkward. She helped me get off on the right foot about selling. It paid a fourth of a week's lodging and made me see that there was more to be had from painting than the pleasure and relief of doing it. I gave Sarah shelter and food for half a week with that picture. The joy of giving to her from my inheritance had not prepared me for the joy of giving her what I earned. There was no comparison.

While I have Sarah's lap to drop my money into, I can never tire of selling.

One morning in mid-May Sarah asked me to come with her. She had made, if I would agree, a choice. "The house needs work," she said. "I don't know you'll like it."

I thought I'd made it clear that I'd agree to any place by then, especially with so much of our money spent and both her dresses somewhat horsey however much I aired them. But she said, no, I had to see the place before she could be definite.

We hired a horse and buggy and drove out the turnpike to Freehold, which was fifteen miles. Oh what a lovely bright pure young green morning it was. Even our tired livery horse could feel the hope of such a morning and clip along. The mountains were like lady giants lying together, vast hips and breasts. The fruit trees were in flower.

At Freehold we stopped for the owner of the farm. His name was Mr. More and he owned several farms. He and his sons farmed ours and pastured here in summer, but nobody lived here.

We drove a short way up the narrow rutty spur called Red Mill Road, and here we were.

Sarah had not exaggerated. Yes, the house needed work.

"I didn't mention, it's logs," she said.

"So I see."

She stayed in the buggy with Mr. More while I looked around the house. It was simply an old abandoned log cabin left from the time when the frontier was here. So many times I'd described log cabins and how to build them to my pupils, but this was the first one I ever actually saw. It was the size I'd told my pupils was usual—twenty by sixteen, roughly. Poor old relic, easing its way back to earth. The ridgepole sagged like a rope between the gables. Someone had long since taken the door for its boards. The windows were empty holes, without even sashes. The chimney was at least stone, not mud and sticks, but it was cracked and partly fallen.

I went inside. All the leaves and dust from forty acres were blown into the corners. There were even a few weeds growing in the deepest parts. The floor was split logs— puncheons—flat side up, laid none too fussily. There was evidence that Mr. More's cattle had found shelter here. I saw sunbeams coming through the roof and between most of the logs.

I went back to the buggy.

"How much?" I asked.

"Just what I told your sister: six-forty," Mr. More said.

I looked at Sarah. "Can you make something of the fields?" I asked.

"I think so."

Mr. More said, "A little chinking—some quarrels in the windows—some jacking—"

I turned my back and walked away. How dared he tell me what to do? I knew what to do. Nobody has to tell me how to run my home.

We all three drove back to Kaatskill and did the legal things at bank and courthouse. Six hundred and forty, when we'd been ready to go to eight! It was like a gift of a hundred and sixty dollars.

By two in the afternoon we had our indenture, and our earnest paid, and Edward written to for more, and our lodging dismissed. We were on a dray with our trunks, heading home along the turnpike. We had broom and hoe and scrubbing brush and pail and mortar and ax and saw and boards and nails and windows, and a great marvelous mess to use them on. Food too. Lots of things. Twine, curtain cloth, rope, a ton of wonders.

Mr. More said, "I don't know how I'll find time to help you. Me and the boys've got our own cornland to work up. It's a poor time for a bee."

"Don't think of it, Mr. More," I said.

But with what guilt they set us down and left us here alone, our drayman and Mr. More. The more we said we'd be just fine, the more it proved we didn't know. They kept looking back doubtfully. We waved and smiled each time.

Then they were out of sight, and the world was out of sight, and right there in the wide-open of our yard Sarah held me close and kissed me.

We had to begin with a kiss, of course. Anything else

would have been improper. But we made it a short one. Our new home was more exciting.

"Here we are," I said.

"Let me out of this *dress,*" Sarah said.

We had about three hours of daylight left. There was no really correct place to begin. Anywhere would do, but Sarah decided the roof was most important.

She cut and trimmed a small tree to prop the ridge-pole. In fact, she cut two; the first she cut too short. The second was too long, but she chopped bits off until it could be jammed and clouted and pried into place, upright in the middle of the floor. It gave us, so to speak, a four-room house. The ridgepole seemed to consider crumbling into dust at the shock, but it settled down still in place. I knew that was a good omen.

Sarah seemed to think it meant we could sleep inside the house right away, but I went ahead with making our first home in the neat orderly out-of-doors.

I gathered dry leaves and pine needles and some last year's cornhusks and stuffed the empty tick I'd brought from Connecticut. Our trunks made an open-sided square around our camp, and then I roofed them with hemlock branches arranged more or less like thatch. I kindled fire with flint and steel, though it would have been quicker to walk to Freehold after coals. It was important that our first fire be original. Our own pure creek was handy-by to give me water for a stew. While it cooked I went to work scraping the cabin floor with our new hoe. Sarah had to rest awhile and gaze at her pole. "Just can't take my eyes off it," she admitted.

Mr. More came by when he'd finished his supper. He seemed disappointed to find us so cozy and cheerful, sitting on our tick and quilts and eating our good-smelling supper from two pretty plates and cups with two silver spoons. What a beautiful word "two" is.

"Where'd you get that fire?" he asked. "*I* fetched you some."

"How kind of you," I said.

"And my wife sends you bread and salt. I'll make you the loan of any tool I'm not using myself. You ladies sisters?"

"Not exactly."

"You kin at all?"

"In a way."

"Where be ye from?"

I had no reason not to tell. I just didn't like being questioned. "We're Yankees," I said.

He was kind and we needed him, but I was glad to have him go.

A better guest came later, as I was settling my back into Sarah's front to fall asleep. We heard a noise and sat up so fast we jarred the hemlock thatch. It was a dog, a big male pup almost grown, black and white and ruddy brown, with ears lopped over at the tips and a white plumed tail that curled over and rested on his back. He was about a foot and a half tall at the shoulder.

We fed him stew. That's when his tail curled over.

"I wonder whose he is," I said.

"He's ours, because he came to us," Sarah said. We named him George.

In the night, George growled softly. Sarah crawled out and listened. "It's just critters. They've had the run of the place so long they can't get used to it we belong here now," she said, in a voice clear and loudish, to let them know they had to stay away. I built up the fire.

George settled down again, so we did. "First thing the store opens, I'll buy a gun," Sarah said.

I didn't wholly like having George on our quilt, but he felt he had a natural right to it and perhaps he did. He was never an unmixed blessing, but there was reassurance in his weight and warmth on our feet that night, and in his animal alertness, and maybe even in his maleness. I wouldn't rule it out.

Sarah was still preoccupied with the roof. She nailed cleats to a pole to make a ladder and climbed up. She poked and tested and considered and came down, not disheartened, to say, "Well, she can't be patched. There's nothing sound to nail to. I've got to put new rafters in and boards and shingles and just make a new one, that's all."

I'd taught my pupils that it takes several men to roof a cabin. I'd also taught them that the weight of the roof is what holds the gable-ends in place. I couldn't swear any of it was true, but it was what I'd taught, and I did dread having our gables topple with everything else we had to do.

"Sarah?"

"Don't stop me now," she said. "This'll take a while. I got to get right at it."

"Sarah, let's hire it done?"

"Hire it!"

But I wore her down with kisses (which George wanted to get in on) and little pouts and by repeating that I *knew* she could do the roof. I said I only wanted to be humored, unreasonably, lovingly indulged, and when she walked into Greenville for the gun she spoke to the storekeeper about a carpenter. (We're about halfway between Freehold and Greenville here, handy to both.) She wore a dress. I thought it best.

The storekeeper himself was a part-time carpenter. That same day he brought out a helper and a wagonload of supplies. They set to with energy and practiced skill, but they were three days at it even so. I thought Sarah might pale a bit at the sight of what she almost undertook to do alone. I was ready to reassure her that she really could have, but the question never came up. She did complain that they'd taken down the ridgepole she'd made such a good prop for, but that was all. My darling does not lack for belief in herself. Even when I can't easily share it, I'm glad she has it.

Except for corn, our fields were already planted, growing oats and potatoes and hay. The cornfield was already prepared. Sarah walked to the red mill our road was named for and carried home a sack of seed corn over her shoulder.

From the pole ladder where I was mortaring first the chimney and then the walls, I could look over the rise behind our house and see my Sarah planting corn, a sight so beautiful I hoped the roofers weren't looking at her too. In her left hand she carried a stick, crossbarred to make a hole of the proper depth. With her right hand she tossed the kernel into the hole and then with a forward step both closed the hole and prepared a new one. Whenever her toss went wrong she bent and saved the kernel. She could go whole rows without having to bend, and even her bending was lovely. In all she planted four acres without an awkward movement and without strain. She said it was sport.

The first cash product of our farm was a wolf. That was while we still slept outside. George sensed it first and woke us. Sarah saw its eyes reflecting our campfire and aimed and fired while I was still looking around for what had wakened George. Sarah is a very good shot, and she'd been practicing, but I think there was some plain good luck involved as well, because wolves are rare here now and such as escape the bounty hunters are careful and wise. And this wolf was at what it must have considered a safe distance. She got it neatly, I'm glad to say. She felt proud, but I was careful not to overpraise that side of her. I'm not really interested in shooting and blood. Next day she took the tail to the town clerk in Greenville and collected a forty-dollar bounty. It paid for our new roof, and I *am* interested in *that*.

We'd been here a week when we moved inside. The corn was planted, the garden was planted. And now we too were planted, to see what grew of us. Our house had a fireplace safe for fire. The floor, though still jaggedy, was scrubbed and bare. Most of the walls were newly chinked. Everything else could wait for the slow quiet steady loving work we longed to give, now that we could pray for rain like any other farmers. Let it come down.

Nothing was urgent then except keeping George out. Sarah cleated three boards together and made a door which she cut and fit until the sagged-in doorframe could contain it. That should have been enough, but with a tall dog like George we needed windows too. He put his elbows on the window sill and walked his hind legs up the wall and burst in delighted with himself, as if to say, see, folks, you needn't have worried.

The window frames were as out-of-true as the door. By the sheerest grace of God the sashes we'd bought were too small, and Sarah was able to stuff wedges and scraps of wood around them and mortar them into place.

And George was out, to stay. He couldn't believe it. Hadn't he practically bought our roof by telling Sarah about the wolf? Hadn't he let *us* sleep with *him*? He barked imperiously. He whined forlornly. We swatted him, and Sarah had long talks with him, and I gave him the quilt I'd made at age thirteen. (He'd dirtied it anyway.) I don't know which worked. Sarah thinks it was her talks. She thinks he was quick-witted and reasonable. I won't go into that. But I think it was the swats. Somehow it got to him that there was not just some awful oversight, that we intended to do him as we did, and that we would not relent. He decided to forgive us and sleep on the quilt outside. In time Sarah made him a house of his own. We did need him. We did love him. Just not in the bodily way he thought at first. Some people claim to have dogs who consider themselves human. I claim of George that he thought we were dogs.

So we were in and there was time for everything. I said, "What would I do, if the wash were done and the curtains made and the potatoes hoed and the walls plastered and the shelves made and the dishes on them? If *everyt*hing were done, what would I do?" I thought a while. "If everything were done, I'd bake you a cake, sweetheart."

And I beat one together, quick as *that*, even without a table to set the bowl on. I used a trunk top. Sarah sat leaned against a wall watching me. I pretended to have forgotten her. I made little humming noises, all artless and unaware.

She made me feel so beautiful and interesting and that I did everything just right, all the correct methods.

She made me feel like the Lord's High Priestess, the Channel of Holy Mysteries, the Eternal Mother, the Bringer of All Good Gifts.

Ah, Sarah, in your eyes I see myself become what I always dreamed I could be.

When the cake was in the oven, making beauty for the nose, I said, "*Now* what would I do, if everything were done? I'd make a special painting for our home."

"I'd build us a bed," Sarah said, "if I could part from you."

"Why part?"

"Outside the door. So far," she said. "Where I can't see you paint or smell the cake."

"Nothing to do but build it here beside me."

"You wouldn't like the mess."

"Nothing to do but love the mess, if you make it."

Time modified my feeling there, but that day I did love the sawdust and the chips she made. For materials she had the poles she'd cut to prop the roof, and some others she'd meant for firewood.

I painted Boaz and Ruth and Naomi, Boaz distant, very small, his back turned, leaving. I call it, "Where Thou Lodgest, I Will Lodge." I meant it to be the central ornament of our home, but it got a little out of hand. Even its basis in Scripture could not make the embrace of Ruth and Naomi spiritual enough for guests to see. Yet, although I soon saw that the painting would be unsuitable, I went ahead with it. The new colors I'd bought in New York were so exciting. rich and brilliant. I could hardly pause to have a piece of cake. The painting took me most of the day and I got a good do on it. It glows.

Sarah finished the bedstead, a shaggy rectangular frame on shaggy cornerposts. A cabinetmaker would have frowned. The thought of his frown made us laugh. We made a web of ropes stretched tight. On went the lumpy tick. On went the bridal sheets of fine linen from my hope chest, the Tree of Life quilt that was my grandmother's. Our bed was made. We stood holding hands admiring it. "O beautiful! O beautiful!" we said.

We lay down to test it and to begin our feast of love. I kissed her and enfolded her, fully trusting our hearts to flood us and our toes to curl. It was time for our feast, to have all we wanted, to be wild and careless and noisy and free. I would shout my triumph when Sarah groaned. I would groan for her. We would make the bed gallop. The floor would ring like a drum. ·

All that was to be, but not then. I watched her for the little pause, the little central stillness, the soft blurriness in her eyes, that would mean we were starting up. They didn't come. I could not have been more surprised if my voice had failed me. I kept on kissing her. What was wrong? Had she set her will against me? No, her face was beautifully tender, full of love. I knew mine must be too.

What was it? Had we forsaken all of our duties and passed the whirlpool at Hell Gate, and faced death by exploding steam, and slept on the ground in the rain, for a feeling not very pressing, not very important? I remembered what Edward had said about the length of woman's love. I remembered Sarah's fears that we would be only friends. Was this what we'd climbed the thorny mountain for?

I was afraid. "Give! Give!" I said. "How can I feel

when you won't feel?" My kiss was harsh. Often she liked it harsh, but this time she turned her face away.

"I can't. Not right now," she said. "And you can't, either."

"We *can!* We've *got* to! We've got to start our bed right!"

She smiled and I listened to what I'd said and felt foolish but managed to smile too. She was full of laugh, but held back not to hurt me, but she let it roll when I began to laugh.

I tried to get off her and couldn't and we found that our weight had stretched our web of ropes into a sort of hanging pocket, very like the nest of a yellow robin.

So what our bed first shook from was laughter. We laughed so hard we could hardly climb out.

Finally, of course, we did get out, and we lifted off the bedclothes and tick and took a look at the ropes and fell to laughing again.

Then Sarah said, "Nothing to do but do it right. I hoped I needn't."

I should have known the web wouldn't work. After all, I was the one who'd had a real bed before and a bed-wrench to keep it taut. Sarah hadn't. But I'd hoped too.

We were so glad through that whole time to have no one around to see our mistakes. We were free to remember and invent with no one to say our ways would never do. Sometimes, indeed, our ways did fail. But often they did not.

Sarah walked to Freehold to return Mr. More's chisels and borrow his auger, and to buy bedcord.

While she was gone I started making curtains. We worked through what remained of daylight, and then on and on by firelight. When we got hungry we finished off the cake. It felt so good to be naughty unwholesome children, eating what was tempting and not getting sensible rest. Sarah was boring holes and whittling pegs, stringing the bed up properly. Naturally she couldn't bear to stop, any more than I could leave the curtain-making. The first curtain was so bright and lovely against the brown logs of the wall. Making the others went more slowly, because I had to keep gazing up at what was already done.

What a sweet night it was, of quiet work and talk. I loved it for itself and for being the pattern of all the time to come. Work is endless and we could never lack for topic: I had my whole life and every thought and fear and wish to tell, and hers to hear, and every day would bring more.

We worked until our eyes felt small and gritty and we ached all over from sitting on the floor. Against our wishes we had to stop. Sarah so much wanted to finish the bed, but we had to bed down on the floor.

Almost yawning, I leaned for our goodnight kiss, meant to be quick and soft. It was soft, but long. I have no way of knowing how long.

Strange of our feeling, to refuse to be summoned when it would have been so welcome and appropriate, to dedicate our bed, and then to seize us by surprise, uninvited.

It has so often been that way, our hearts cool at times when heat would have been ceremonially correct and then flaming up when we couldn't really spare the time and strength. We have thought about that strangeness a lot and talked about it together. We needed words for it. I used to say, "It is as though love holds us, not we it." I used to say, "See how our blessing suits not our convenience but its own."

It was Sarah who finally found the words.

She said, "You can't tell a gift how to come."

AFTERWORD

This story was suggested by the life of the painter Mary Ann Willson and her companion Miss Brundidge, who lived and farmed together for many years on Red Mill Road, Greenville Town, Greene County, New York State, in the early part of the nineteenth century.

Not much is left of them. Even their hill—still called Brundage—is partly gone, bulldozed for road improvement. I couldn't find them in any Greene County census, or in the records of land transactions in the Catskill courthouse.

Still, something is left. The bright, playful watercolors are left. And "Admirer of Art," a friend, wrote a note about Miss Willson and Miss Brundidge. It's safe in a book.[1] What looks to be Admirer of Art's first draft is safe in the Vedder Library of the Greene County Historical Society at Coxsackie, New York. There is another account in a book called *Picturesque Catskills*.[2]

So we know about their "romantic attachment" to each other, their quiet peaceful life, the respect and help of their neighbors, their dooryard full of flowers, their plowing and haying, their cow, the improvised paints—berries and brick dust—the paintings sold for twenty-five cents to neighbors or bartered to peddlers who carried them all over eastern North America, from Canada to Mobile. And we know our own response. We are provoked to tender dreams by a hint. Any stone from their hill is a crystal ball.

—ISABEL MILLER

1. Lipman, Jean, and Black, Mary C. *American Folk Painting*. New York: C. N. Potter, 1966.
2. DeLisser, R. Lionel. *Picturesque Catskills*. Northampton, Mass.: Picturesque Publishing Co., 1894. Reprinted 1967 by Hope Farm Press, Cornwallville, N.Y.